H. P Fitch

Through shadow to sunshine

H. P Fitch

Through shadow to sunshine

ISBN/EAN: 9783744740890

Printed in Europe, USA, Canada, Australia, Japan

Cover: Foto ©Andreas Hilbeck / pixelio.de

More available books at **www.hansebooks.com**

THROUGH

SHADOW

TO

SUNSHINE.

~~~~~~~~~~~~~~~~~~

FITCH.

~~~~~~~~~~~~~~~~~~

"No man shall arise in the judgment and say 'Doctor Benjamin Rush made me a drunkard.'"

—Doctor Rush in 1775.

HASTINGS, NEBRASKA.
GAZETTE-JOURNAL COMPANY.
1885.

TO THE MEMORY OF
MY FATHER,
WHO, THOUGH HE HAS ENTERED INTO
THE REST THAT REMAINETH,
STILL LIVES
IN HIS LOVING COUNSELS AND PIOUS EXAMPLES,
AND TO
MY MOTHER,
AT WHOSE KNEE I EARLY LEARNED
THOSE PURE PRINCIPLES
WHICH HAVE BEEN THE GUIDE AND SAFEGUARD
OF MY LIFE, THIS LITTLE OFFERING IS
AFFECTIONATELY DEDICATED BY
THE AUTHOR.

CONTENTS.

PREFACE.

———

For a number of years the Author of this little volume has been in the habit of keeping a memorandum of the various incidents coming under his own observation, illustrative of the laws regulating the traffic in intoxicating drinks. In the following pages he has endeavored to weave these various incidents into the form of a simple story, in the hope that it may aid those who are so earnestly striving to save our country from this great national evil.

He is fully conscious of its many demerits as a literary effort, and trusts this frank acknowledgement will, as much as is proper, disarm criticism. It has been written at odd times, snatched from the most possible busy, active life, in many cases during hours that should have been devoted to sleep. The scenes are mostly given just as he knew them in some cases not even the name being changed.

With an earnest prayer that it may accomplish its purpose, that by it some weak ones may be strengthened, and sorrowing ones be encouraged to labor and to hope, he sends it forth on its humble mission.　　　H. P. F.

Through Shadow to Sunshine.

CHAPTER I.

THE STUDENTS.

In a small, plainly furnished room in the second story of a house, in one of our beautiful eastern cities sat, in earnest conversation, the two friends, Harry Ferguson and Harry Wardsworth. They had met together to spend their last evening, before passing out from their student life to meet the sterner duties of their profession. They had not only been fast friends, but had been both room and classmates, through all their course, in that pride of American culture, Yale College.

Now, their course was completed, and however firm and lasting their friendship, their paths in life, must, from this point diverge.

They had graduated with the highest honors of their class, had delivered their graduating orations, had listened to the parting advice and counsel of the President, and had met in their room, to spend together their last evening, before going out into the world, each one to take his own way, and, though in different fields, to engage in the great battle of life.

It was a deeply interesting hour to the two friends. It was the hour in which they took a review of the past, and with earnest eye, sought to scan the future. Their friendship had been such as is only formed in college halls. Well fitted, each to attract the other, they had early been drawn together by mutual tastes and aims, and their friendship had deepened with every year of their acquaintance.

They had been members of the law department, and had labored to thoroughly prepare themselves for the duties of their profession. And certainly, among all those who were to go out from those college halls, no two students gave better promise of future success. Well read in legal lore, with a mind trained to close thought, and a power of concentration possessed by few, combined with an eloquent delivery, all who had the pleasure of their acquaintance predicted for them a most brilliant future.

In size and form they were much alike. Standing nearly six feet, well proportioned, with a noble, manly bearing, they were men who would attract attention, even in a multitude. Ferguson was the senior of his friend by one year, having reached the age of twenty-five.

"So you have finally decided to follow the setting sun and pitch your tent in Cedarville?" remarked Ferguson to Wardsworth, as he helped himself to a glass of wine and then passed the decanter to his companion.

"Yes, Ferguson, I have decided to try it

there," replied Wardsworth as he filled his glass; "it is a beautiful little city of about ten thousand, and is, withal, a most thriving place. As I have told you before, on the death of my parents, I became possessed of a little money, sufficient to purchase me a nice residence, and I do not know of a better place to invest it than in Cedarville. I propose, after a time, to secure me a good home, and, settling down to hard, earnest work, do my best to honor the profession I have chosen. But you have not yet told me anything concerning your plans."

"No, for the simple reason that I have none. I shall fulfill a promise I have made my parents to go home and visit, and recruit for a few weeks, and, in the meantime, look around. I have thought some of going into the State of ———, and hanging out my shingle in some of the new towns springing up there, but I have not yet decided. Were I to do so, we would not be quite as far apart as if I remained in the East. One thing is certain, Wardsworth, there is room for us, as one of the great men said, 'in the upper story,' and I for one am going to make an effort to climb up there. We shall both make our mark somewhere, I hope. You have the advantage of me a little, in having some money to start with. I have nothing but willing hands and a determined spirit, but these are enough in this country, to enable a man to succeed. I shall expect to see the name of Harry Wardsworth written, in a few years, very high up in the list of America's brilliant lawyers, and, perhaps, statesmen."

"As to that I cannot say, Ferguson, I certainly intend to do my best, and I have high hopes of accomplishing some good while I live. I think I can say that simply making money, or merely a living, was not, by any means, the primary object I had for choosing the profession of law. The power of doing good; of espousing the cause of the weak against the strong; the satisfaction of sometimes being able to protect the oppressed against the tyranny and injustice of the oppressor—for, you know, we have these things, even in our own land— . has weighed as much with me in making my choice, as anything else. One thing I have resolved never to do, let the consequence be what it may, and that is to degrade my profession by espousing an unrighteous cause for the sake of gain."

"A noble resolution, truly, Wardsworth, and one I hope we shall both be able to carry out. The law can either be made a power for good, or, a mighty instrument of evil, and which, depends on the disposition and motives of the man who wields it. And yet, I apprehend we shall have some difficulty in carrying out these resolutions. I can easily imagine cases in which we may be perfectly satisfied of the justice of our cause, and yet be mistaken. There is where those fine powers of perception, the possession of which I have sometimes almost envied you, will serve you a noble purpose. When do you leave for Cedarville?"

"To-morrow evening. I am somewhat impatient to get there and get to work. I hope, Ferguson, wherever you settle, the friendship that has been so warm during our college life will not be allowed to grow cold by our contact with the sterner duties of our profession."

"I most cordially reciprocate that wish my dear friend, but our country is so large, and our professional men acquire the habit of such close application to business, that it will not be much wonder if we drift apart, save, perhaps, as we occasionally cross each other's path in the swift journey through life. Ah, well! I suppose it must be so, and I am ready to assume my share of life's burdens; but, as far as enjoyment is concerned, I could be very well satisfied to spend a few years in old Yale yet."

Thus the two friends continued their conversation till past the hour of midnight. There was so much of the past to be recalled, so much of the future to be explored. What plans they laid! What high and lofty purposes they expressed! What noble resolutions they formed, and strove to strengthen each other to carry them out! How grand and noble life appeared to them as they looked off into the future! Oh! could they have lifted the curtain and read all of their future life, could they have known all, how they would have shrunk back dismayed! Could they have seen all the bitter heart struggles, the blasted hopes, the blighted prospects, the withered joys! But they could not; and so, full of that ardent enthusiasm, that throbs in the breast of every young man who makes his mark in life, they resolutely prepared to buckle on their armor and go forth to fight life's battle. Will they be able to carry out all those noble resolutions? Will they realize all their bright anticipations? Fair and beautiful appears their barque as she turns her prow toward the other shore. Will she nobly defy the storm and the tempest, or will she, with dismantled rigging, go down beneath the angry billows? We shall see.

The next day was spent by Wardsworth in making a few calls on personal friends, and packing his trunks for his departure. The nine o'clock bell struck as the train which was to bear him away reached the depot. With a last shake of the hand, and amid many wishes for future success, the friends separated, and Wardsworth turned his face toward the setting sun, to carve out for himself a name and a destiny.

CHAPTER II.

THE WEDDING.

Three years have elapsed since the events narrated in the last chapter, and we find ourselves in the beautiful city of Cedarville, in the State of ——. Wonderful indeed has been the progress of the city during those three years. Its population has increased from between ten and twelve thousand to over fifteen thousand, with all the advantages and improvments of a city of the first-class. As we walk along its finely paved streets and admire its large and costly brick blocks, we instinctively exclaim: "How wonderful is this growing West!"

On one of the most prominent business streets, on the ground floor of an imposing and handsome block, we notice a large and attractive looking office. We pause and read on the nicely painted shingle, "Harry Wardsworth, Attorney-at-Law." At once we are reminded that three years ago this was the city toward which the young lawyer looked from the halls of his *Alma Mater*.

So far he has succeeded beyond his most sanguine expectations. Possessed of a brilliant intellect, a fine personal appearance, extensive erudition, and a gift of eloquence excelled by few, he had at once taken his place among the foremost lawyers of the State. He has invested his money prudently, and is now the happy possessor of one of the most beautiful and costly residences, on one of the finest streets of the city. At present he has gone East on important business, whither we will follow him.

It was a bright, glad May morning in one of the interior cities of the State of New York. Nature had put on her most beautiful robes, as if in anticipation of the happy event which was that day to be consummated. Never had the birds sung more sweetly. Never had the flowers bloomed more beautifully, nor given forth a more delightful fragrance. Never had the sun shone more brightly. So thought Belle Hargrave, as she looked forth from her chamber window, and, with a heart full of glad hope, contemplated all the varied scenes of beauty by which she was surrounded And gladly did her own heart respond to the voice of Nature in rendering praise to the Giver of all good. To her this is to be *the* day of all the days of her life: it is her marriage day. This is the day she is to publicly plight her vows of life-long devotion to the man of her choice, "For better, for worse, till Death do us part." With what eager joy she seeks to scan the future! As she looks forth on all the beautiful picture Nature's hand has painted, she exclaims, "How beautiful is earth! How bright and cloudless are the skies! Even so, Father," she added reverently, "if it be Thy will, may the sky of my life be ever bright, until its sun goes peacefully down without a cloud to obscure its departing rays."

And she truly believed it would be so. Even so does the hand of Destiny hide from our eyes the book of fate. What mattered it to her, though she had spent the last night in the dear old home that had ever been her shelter and refuge! That henceforth that dear house, with all its pleasant associations, was to be her home no more. That the kind and loving parents, whose gentle hand had so tenderly led her, should no more be her guardians, her guide. That this day she is to go to a land of strangers, having taken upon herself the solemn vows of wife! True, she felt sad at the thought of leaving her parents all alone. That she could no more be permitted to soothe their cares or minister to the wants of their declining years. That they could no more listen to her voice in song, or her merry laugh, save as they came to them in their dreams of night. But, for herself, there was no thought of sorrow. Fancy painted the future in such glowing colors, that her heart's only wish was to hasten forth to meet her life's destiny.

Ah! well it is for us that we cannot read all the future. That Fancy's hand so gently touches the canvas, on which is painted the scenes of our life's destiny, that all the lines are fair, and all the picture beautiful. What heart would be brave, or what feet could steadily tread the pathway, did we but know of all the thorns by which they are to be lacerated? Happily for us we do not, and so, with a brave heart and a steady purpose, we press on, and when the way grows rough and our feet grow weary, a gift of strength is imparted by which we may still overcome.

A rap at the door aroused Belle Hargrave from her reverie, and, hastening to open it, her sister Kate entered. "Good morning, sister Belle," said her visitor, as she planted a kiss upon the cheek of the fair young girl. For answer, Belle threw her arms around her sister's neck, and looking up into her face, said, "Oh! Kate, I am so happy. Do you think it possible that anybody else could be as happy as I am?"

"I doubt if any other bride elect would be as thoughtless as you are," she answered, returning her salutation. "Here it is after seven o'clock and Harry is to be here at ten. Come, let your castle building rest for awhile and bring yourself down to the matter of fact business of dressing yourself for your intended marriage." Thus admonished, the younger sister allowed herself to be seated, while the elder one began to array her for the ceremony that so soon was to make her the wife of Harry Wardsworth.

"Do you know, Kate," continued Belle, as the sister went on with her toilet, "I never thought I could be any happier than I have been here, with you and our dear parents. I am almost surprised at my own capacity for happiness."

"True, sister," replied Kate, "every new joy develops some new capacity to retain it, as every new sorrow develops some new power to endure it. Very happy indeed does the future appear to you, my dear sister, but it is well to bear in mind that it is not always the brightest morning that gives us the most cloudless day. While I would not cast a shadow over your pathway, I would suggest that it is better to be prepared to meet the shadows, and then, if your life be all sunshine, so much the more will you enjoy it.

"True, sister, but is it not better, instead of borrowing trouble, to enjoy whatever of happiness there is in the present, and if the future bring sorrow, to meet it nobly and bravely?"

"Most certainly, Belle, I would not have you borrow trouble, as you term it, but, oftentimes, by looking ahead we can see where trouble lies, and, by a judicious course, shun it."

"Why, Kate, you cannot possibly see any trouble in my future, can you? Am I not to have one of the noblest and best of men for my husband? Am I not to have one of the most beautiful homes (you know I showed you a pho tograph of it), and everything to make me comfortable and happy? What more can a' woman ask or wish?"

"True, sister, and I do earnestly pray that your fondest anticipations may be realized. But you will admit that I am three years your senior, and have been two years married already, so I have had a .little more experience than you. And I tell you this, dear Belle, there is no home into which there does not enter a shadow. It will enter your home, in some form or another, for every human.life is made up of a mixture of sunshine and shadow."

"And pray, you dearest and best sister," replied Belle, looking up with an arch smile, "look along the pathway on which I am so soon to enter, and see if you can discern any clouds or shadows there."

"There is but one cloud that I can discern in all the sky of your life, so far as I am able to scan it," replied the elder sister, and her voice became grave, almost to sadness.

"And what is that, dear Kate," she asked with a sudden pain at her heart.

"I am told your intended husband has one habit of which I wish he was dispossessed." she added with earnestness.

" Oh! I know what you mean. You refer to his habit of drinking wine, do you not? I ad.

mit, Kate, if it were possible for anything to make me happier than I am now, it would be the assurance that Harry never tasted liquor of any kind; but I have so much love for him and so much confidence in him that I have no fears for the result. He is the very soul of honor, and loves me most devotedly, and this, I am sure, will help to keep him from temptation. Besides, Kate, you know how firmly we have been taught to believe in the power of prayer. I do believe in it, and this is the strong ground of my hope. I have resolved to rely on this in every time of trial, even supposing trials do come."

"You cannot tell, dear sister, how I rejoice to hear you say so; for I do assure you, there is no refuge from sorrow like this. While I do earnestly hope that your future life may be all your fancy has pictured it, I do know, and it may grieve you to say this, no man can continue the habit of liquor drinking without falling, more or less, beneath its power. And when once he has fallen, how very seldom, may I not say never, has he the power to rise, only as he is lifted by a Power from on high."

"But surely, dear Kate, you don't think there is any danger of Harry, do you?" and the tears came into her eyes. "You almost frighten me, your words are so solemn-"

"I have not said there is danger in his case; and yet, for your sake, I wish he were entirely

free from the habit.   More than that, Belle, I
wish his feet were planted on the same Rock
on which you and I have been enabled to take
refuge.   I wish he were a temperance man and
a Christian, then I believe I could rejoice for
you with a full heart."

"Well, Kate, since you have spoken so freely,
I, too, could wish it were otherwise; but I cannot
believe there is danger and have even laughed
at my own fears.   I do not now believe there
is danger.   True, Harry is not a Christian,
though he seems good enough to be one, but he
likes Christian people, and has taken a pew in
the church.   He knows I am a Christian, or trying to be one, and says he loves me all the better for it.   I have thought all these things
over," with a pure earnest look into the face of
her sister, "and I have made my choice.   If sorrow comes I shall pray God to give me a brave heart
and a patient spirit.   This cup of joy has been
placed to my lips, and I will not make its contents bitter by anticipation.   On one thing,
however, I am firmly resolved: Never by word
or act will I countenance the use of liquor in
any way.   I have told Harry this, and he heart-
ily approves my decision."

"I am so thankful to hear you say that, Belle!
You are starting right.   Keep to that resolution,
and then, whatever comes, you cannot reproach
yourself for being, in part, the cause of your own
sorrow.   Oh! how many a wife, and mother too

as they have wept over the dishonored graves of their loved ones, have found their bitterest sorrow in the reflection that they have, with their own hands, sown the seeds from which they are reaping a harvest of misery. Keep faithfully to the course you have marked out, and, with God's blessing, you may hope for a prosperous and happy life."

At that moment a carriage drew up at the front gate, and through the shutters the sisters saw the bridegroom elect, Harry Wardsworth, alight, and hastened their preparations.

The hour of ten found a goodly number of relatives and friends assembled in the parlors of the Hargrave residence, to witness the marriage of the fair Belle. She had grown up from infancy in their midst and was a general favorite with all. They had known her, only to love her. She was so full of innocent mirth, of joyous activity, and, withal, so kind and gentle, that she held a large place in the affections of all who knew her.

As she stood there, dressed in her bridal robes, while the aged pastor, who had known her from childhood, pronounced the solemn words, that made one, those two, already united in heart, "henceforth to live, for better, for worse, until death do you part," a look of sublime devotion rested upon her countenance, and she appeared like some angel from a purer, happier clime. She had laid her heart, her *all,*

on the altar of her devotion. Will the sacrifice
be merely consumed? or will the hallowed in-
cense, bearing the fragrance of her love, ascend
to the throne of the Eternal, and move the
heart of God to overshadow her continually
with the blessing of his favor?

The parents of the bride strove to be cheerful, but there were tears on their cheeks, and a
close observer could have detected a look that
told not only of sorrow, at parting from the
child of their affection, but of anxiety, lest this
bright and cloudless morning be but the harbinger of a day of gloom.

The marriage ceremony was ended. The
bridegroom and bride had received the congratulations of their friends, the last meal had been
taken in the dear old home of her childhood,
and Belle Hargrave, now Mrs. Harry Wardsworth, was ready to start on her journey, to her
new home in the distant West. A few moments were spent, at her own request, with her
parents, in the privacy of their own room.
"Let me go," she said, "with my father's voice
in prayer yet sounding in my ears," so, kneeling
down together, the man of God, in tremulous
tones, commended her to the care of a covenant-
keeping Father.

The hour of departure arrived. The last
"God bless and keep you," had been spoken, the
last kiss, the last wave of the handkerchief giv-
en, and Harry Wardsworth and his young wife,

their hearts filled with a glad hope, were away,
alike on their journey of life, and to their home
in the beautiful, though distant west.

CHAPTER III.

GATHERING SHADOWS.

Five years more have elapsed, and again it is
bright, glad spring-time in the beautiful city of
Cedarville. It is the hour of midnight. The
restless activity of business, and the busy hum
of industry have given place to the silence of
rest and repose. Night has come down and re-
leased the rich man from his business and the
poor man from his toil. The lights are extin-
guished, and the city is in darkness, save here
and there, where some lone watcher keeps his
vigil beside the couch of suffering, or awaits
the coming of a belated traveller; or, it may be,
the noisy reveler still continues his revelry and
dissipation, and foolish man "puts an enemy in
his mouth to steal away his brains."

On one of the most fashionable streets stands
a beautiful and costly residence, in which the
lights are still burning. In the sitting room an
anxious watcher sadly waits the return of one
who is dearer to her than life. Hour after hour
through the long evening has she waited, listening to the tramp of hurrying feet, as they

hastened to the quiet and rest of home, until the last hurrying traveller has passed, and still, her husband comes not.

"Twelve o'clock and Harry not home yet! Oh! how can I endure this agony?" and the wife of only five short years throws herself, in the hopelessness of her grief, on the sofa, and gives way to a flood of tears:

"What have I done to cause this great sorrow! Why have I been thus robbed of my husband's love? But no! I will not believe he has lost his affection for the wife of his choice. Oh! it cannot be that he no longer cherishes a love for his wife, and the dear boy who bears his own image and name. Could he but tear away from the influences that surround him! could he but break the chain that binds him! could he have strength to carry out his resolutions, he might even yet recover himself. Oh! God," she cried, "that I could aid him in this! That I could help him break this accursed chain, that he might once more be free. Oh, how helpless I am! I can do nothing but weep and suffer. Nothing! Surely I cannot so soon forget that 'The name of the Lord is a stong tower, whereunto the righteous may flee and be safe.' True there is nothing left me but prayer. That refuge never yet has failed; and to that truest source of comfort I will go; and kneeling down before Him who has said "Come unto me, ye that labor and are heavy laden, and I will give you rest," she poured out her burdened spirit in an agony of supplication. And the Comforter came down, and above the darkness and the storm was heard the voice which stilled the wild waves of Gallilee. "Peace; be still." Her soul understood the word of the Master, and her faith rose up above the lowering clouds and rested on the Divine promises.

Only five short years before, on a bright, glad spring morning, we saw her who now weeps, as she lonely watches, standing, in all the joyousness of her young life, and plighting her vows to the man of her choice. Then all was bright and joyous. Fancy painted her future in the most glowing colors. Hope beckoned her on, and pointed with its radiant finger to brighter scenes beyond. How eagerly she pressed forward to quaff the cup of bliss that Hope held to her lips! How brightly bloomed the flowers along the pathway on which her feet had entered!

But alas! for the heart that trusted. Alas! for the hopes so bright; for the love so devoted and the man so noble! With all that joyous sunshine, the shadow was even then gathering. One little cloud appeared on the horizon, so small as to be almost imperceptible by one whose hope was so buoyant, and whose love was so pure. As we have seen, Harry Wardsworth had learned to "look upon the wine when it was red." Secure in the consciousness of his

own strength, he had not dreamed of danger.
Generous to a fault, he had been confiding and
trusting, where he ought to have been suspi-
cious and guarded. Little by little, slowly but
surely, the deadly serpent had wound around
him his fatal coils. Tighter and firmer had he
bound him until at last the victim lay helpless
at the mercy of his foe.

The devoted young wife, ever watchful for
him she loved, saw the danger, and faithfully
sounded the alarm. With a voice made tremulous by her fears and her devotion, she, at
first, reasoned, then plead, and then as the
cloud grew larger, and the shadow deeper, with
strong supplication, she besought him, for the
love he bore her, to grapple manfully with his
foe and conquer.

But why need we write the history? It is
but the history of thousands, over all this land.
Every city, every town and village has written
it. In the records of our courts, in the wrecks
that fill our prisons and poor-houses it is written. In the sad-faced widows and orphans,
pinched with starvation and shame, that everywhere meet us, it is written. Above the "low,
silent mounds, where sleep the victims of the
rum traffic," it is written. Yea, it is written in
the book of God's remembrance, recorded there
by an eternal hand.

Harry Wardsworth's history was no exception to the course in all such cases. A history

of a social glass with a friend; of appetite thus formed, of habits that grew stronger, of cravings indulged, of intellect beclouded, honor tarnished and manhood shorn of its strength.

At last there came an awakening; and the heart-rending truth forced itself upon his friends, and ere long upon himself, that Harry Wardsworth was a drunkard. Then there was a repetition af the old history of promises made, only to be broken; of resolutions formed, with no power to carry them out; of falls, and risings up, only to fall again; each time going lower than before; of nights of weary, anxious watching on the part of the wife, and of revelry and dissipation, followed by days of sorrowful regrets, on the part of the husband.

It was indeed, the same old story. Every fall but made him weaker, and his manhood more degraded, until, at last, he seemed to give up all effort to recover himself, and plunged madly into the current, whose dark waters are bearing seventy thousand annually out to the deeper darkness beyond.

This is the reason why she, who, only a few short years ago, was a joyous happy bride, now, with the roses gone from her cheeks, the light of hope from her eye, and sorrow filling her heart, is sitting there, on this May midnight, in the hopelessness of her grief.

But what of the erring husband all this time? Of the once proud and gifted Harry Wardsworth? He had gone out in the early evening, promising to return befor nine. And he had fully intended to do so. But who that is caught in the toils of the Demon of Rum can say where, or how he shall direct his steps? Wardsworth was no exception to the rule. The coils of the serpent were around him, and the victim was led captive at his will. "Just one glass, Harry," said his false friend, as he met him that evening: "Just one glass," answered the craving appetite within, and, in a moment, all his promises and good resolutions were swept away, and the husband whose gentle wife, waited and watched for his coming, held in his hand the cup that sparkles but to kill.

The clock had struck the hour of two, and Mrs. Wardsworth decided to retire. Little Harry had already been put in his crib, the last good-night kiss pressed upon his cheek, the nightly prayer had gone up from the desolate wife, when the sound of voices and confused footsteps fell upon her ear. The steps drew nearer and paused at the door, which was opened, and her husband stood before her in a state of beastly intoxication.

"Do not feel alarmed, madam," said a stranger, who was holding him by the arm; "your husband is all right, He has been spending the evening with some friends, and took a little too much wine. He will be all straight in the morning." To this explanation or apology, the wife made no reply. Too well she knew where he had been, and the influences by which he had been surrounded. She uttered no word of complaint, but a red spot burned on either cheek, as, taking him by the arm, she assisted his unsteady steps to the sofa, on which he threw himself heavily. A few feeble attempts were made at apology, but they were almost unintelligible, and, in a few moments, he was in a sleep so deep, that, only for the dark flush upon his face, he might have been thought dead.

The devoted wife made him as comfortable as possible, and then sat down to meditate, and, if possible, to plan some mode of deliverance. What wonder if memory, with a homesick longing, went back to the joyous days of her girlhood. Back to the dear old eastern home, where "free from sorrow's dull aching," she had nestled. Back over the early years of her married life, when all was bright and beautiful, and no thought of sorrow had yet come. Alas! how sudden and how sad the change.

Slowly passed the hours of night, and still the husband slept, while the wife waited and watched, and pondered. At last the grey dawn stole up from the far east,—the darkness fled from the valleys and the hills—the birds came forth, with their morning song, from their nightly hiding place, and the sun poured its bright beams, into the abode of sorrow, as the wife, weary and prostrate, threw herself on her couch, for a short respite in sleep.

CHAPTER IV.

PLOTTING.

The Honorable Hezekiah Simkins sat lazily in his office watching the wreaths of smoke that floated gracefully up from his cigar, and sadly dreaming of departed glory. To tell the whole truth, the Hon. Hezekiah was in a very unpleasant frame of mind. He was living in the past, as that contained whatever of *respectable* influence he had ever enjoyed, or perhaps ever would. He was a lawyer, not overstocked with brains or learning; but what nature, and the schools, had denied him, in this respect, had been more than compensated by an extraordinary quantity of cheek. He was also blessed with a very fluent tongue, was subtle and cunning, in his way, and boasted of representing in his practice more money than any other lawyer in the city. He was popular with all the saloon-keepers, could take his glass with any of them, could talk politics by the hour to the drunken crowd by whom he was generally surrounded, and was, in all respects, a first-class representative of what is known as a street corner politician.

Some few years before the events recorded in the last chapter, the friends of law and order had united in an effort to secure the passage of a prohibitory liquor law for the State. This had aroused all the energies of the liquor dealers, and forgetting everything else in their desire to save their craft, they resolved to unite in one solid phalanx for the purpose of defeating the temperance measure.

The first step was to secure a candidate for the State legislature who would pledge himself to vote against the measure, in whatever form it might come up, "first, last, and all the time." The name of lawyer Simkins was proposed in convention and received with cheers. In fact, he was the man. He was fond of his glass. The whisky dealers were his clients. His principal support came from that party which, it was argued, gave them a great power over him, and he was, moreover, ambitious of legislative honors. A committee was therefore appointed to wait on him; the pledge was readily given, and Hezekiah Simkins, attorney at law, became the candidate of the whisky party, bound by his pledge of honor, by whatever of personal influence he possessed, and by his own appetites and tastes, to oppose the submitting to a vote of the people any amendment to the constitution looking to the prohibition of the liquor traffic.

Oh! when will the friends of temperance

learn a lesson from their enemies? When will they learn that to succeed in this great conflict between good and evil, between the down-trodden victims of the liquor traffic, and humanity's most deadly foe, they, too, must sink every other political consideration! That members of every political party, of every religious creed, must unite in one determined effort and confining, at least for the present, the fight to the individual States, resolve, that *there* everything else shall bow before this mighty effort for the alleviation of our people.

The fight at Cedarville was indeed a desperate one, as all such fights usually are. On the one side were the lovers of law and order. Christian men, sober, solid business men, the very backbone of the community. Unfortunately, a few temperance men made the fatal mistake that is always made in those contests. Their sympathies were with prohibition, but they did not wish to vote against their political party. The result was, the friends of temperance were pitted not only against their legitimate foes, but against some of their so-called friends as well. They were thus wounded in the house of their friends, besides meeting the whole combined influence of the liquor traffic itself. To the contestants on that side, money was no object, if only they could accomplish their purpose. Every art, both fair and foul, was brought into requisition. Whisky flowed like water, and money was lavished with an unsparing hand. Nevertheless the prohibition party made a most gallant and determined fight; and could they have had the support *of all* of the *temperance men,* would have gained the victory. As it was they were borne down by numbers, and Simkins was elected by a small majority.

The first thing the victorious party did was to celebrate their victory. The saloons were all thrown open and liquor was free. They could afford it, with Simkins elected. Every man was invited to drink. The successful candidate was cheered whenever he appeared. He drank with everybody who invited him. He made speeches whenever called upon to do so. He was first eloquent, then boisterous, then obscene and maudlin, till at last even his system, trained as it was to drinking, was no longer able to withstand the pressure and Hezekiah Simkins, attorney at law, member-elect of the State legislature, the man to whom was entrusted the enactment of laws for two millions of people, was carried home on a shutter in a state of beastly intoxication.

The Hon. Hezekiah faithfully carried out all his pledges. In whatever shape the temperance measure was presented he voted against it. He also kept the whisky men thoroughly posted on all the doings of the temperance party, so far as either by fair means or foul he could learn them, and, without blushing, could boast that he was doing the work of a spy, "free, gratis, for nothing." He gave to the committee of lobbyists the names of all those members whom he had reason to believe could be safely approached for the purchase of their votes. In short, he worked in the house and out of the house, honestly and dishonestly; for the masters to whom he had sold himself body and soul, mentally and politically. And he had his reward; for when the final vote was taken on the question of submitting an amendment to the vote of the people, and it was defeated by a small majority, the whisky dealers again came forward with their money and the Hon.(?) Hezekiah and his friends again celebrated their victory by getting gloriously drunk.

But somehow a change had come over the spirit of his dreams. The very few, who, at first, had supported him from principle, soon became disgusted and withdrew from the party. Others who remained, but who yet possessed the smallest amount of respectability and intelligence, saw that with Simkins for their candidate, they were certain of an inglorious defeat, and used their influence to secure, at least, a more respectable candidate. The result was, that, at the end of the first term, when the convention again assembled for the choice of a candidate, Simkins was defeated by a large majority, and consigned to the cold shades of private life.

Hezekiah Simkins, however, was not a man to forget an injury, nor to even palliate a mistake. He had carefully noted every man who had voted and worked against him, and had vowed revenge against everyone. He never dreamed that they could have been conscientious in what they did. He never fancied, for a moment, that any other man could more intelligently represent the voters of his county than himself. They had all acted, in his estimation, from personal motives. They had acted meanly, and meanness they should have to their heart's content.

Among those who had supported his first nomination, but who had been led to see his danger, and for his own sake, and for the sake of those dear to him, earnestly desired the passage of a prohibitory law, and had therefore withdrawn entirely from the party, was Harry Wardsworth. Against him, therefore, in common with some others, the Hon. Hezekiah had sworn special vengeance, and he only waited a favorable opportunity to put his threat into execution.

We have said that this particular hour, when we introduce him to our readers, he was in a very unpleasant frame of mind. He had been living over again the scenes of the past. He had remembered, oh with what a hungry longing, all the gay scenes he had enjoyed at the capitol. His thoughts fondly dwelt upon the

free drinks and free lunches, and even free
dinners with which he had regaled himself. He
remembered the "fair women and brave men,"
whose acquaintance he had made, and whose
society he had enjoyed.   This part of his meditation was pleasant enough; but, unfortunately
it was followed immediately by the very unpleasant reflection, that, so far as he was concerned. these pleasures had been fleeting as the
mists of the morning.   Had gone, doubtless to
return no more.   Others would stand up and
pour forth their oratory within those halls.
Would mould their wisdom into laws. and place
them on imperishable records.   Would stand
amid the glare of gaslight and by their eloquence, move the multitude at will; would eat
all the ·free dinners and drink all the free
drinks, but the glory of Honorable Hezekiah
Simkins had forever departed; or, in other
words, his political influence had "gone where
the woodbine twineth."

The ex legislator had just reached the point
in his meditation, where for, perhaps, the five
thousandth time he had resolved to wreak his
vengeance, as he expressed it, "on the dastardly
rascals who had dared to go back on him," when
his office door was opened, and in walked his
friend and client, Solomon Slocum, Esq.

Reader, we wish we could give you a description of this gentleman, but, as we are perfectly
incapable of doing the subject justice, we shall

not enter into it farther than to say—imagine a
very large squash, with a very small head on
one end and very short legs on the other, and
you have a tolerably fair representation of his
form. His head was very small, and his body
very short; but then it was large enough in cir-
cumference to make it up. His face was full,
and round and red. His eyes kept a constant
furtive movement, turning suddenly from one
point to another, as though they wanted to
look all ways at once. His nose turned up, as
though it had been trying to get as far as possible from what was going into his mouth.
When he walked, he waddled like a duck, and
when he sat down, he threw his head back,
projected his stomach forward, and puffed, like
a horse that has the heaves and had been driv-
en too fast. His voice was wheezy like that of
a pig when it gets too fat; or like the sound of
a blacksmith's bellows when it gets a hole in it.

Do not let our readers understand us as
wishing to prejudice them against Solomon
Slocum, Esq. We have only endeavored to
give them an idea of his personal appearance.
We admit that, so far as that was concerned,
the combined labors of nature and habit had
resulted in a very bad failure. But Squire
Slocum was a gentleman. He sported a gold-
headed cane, wore a broadcloth suit, patent
leather boots, a shirt with a ruffled front, was
said to be one of the richest men in Cedarville,

and was, moreover, the client and bosom friend of Honorable Hezekiah Simkins. As he very frequently reminded the ex-legislator, "Old Slocum had never gone back on him." Besides this, he boasted that he had risen to opulence by his own exertions.

Slocum's first money was the result of his intense patriotism. At the commencement of the late war he was so very patriotic that he succeeded in enlisting several times and drawing his bounty every time. This had given him sufficient capital to open a small retail saloon. By the judicious use of rain water and certain other ingredients, he had succeeded in getting and saving money enough to build a small brewery. This he had enlarged from time to time until it did a large business. At last he reached, as he said, the goal of his ambition, and was able to build a large distillery. This made a market for grain, and he would have been quite popular had it not been for his avarice.

A year or two before he is introduced to our readers, he had become posessed of a very valuable secret. A secret so valuable that he revealed it to no one, but his sworn and trusty distiller, and they two kept it confined within the darkened cellar, into which no one but themselves were allowed to enter. It was no less, than the art of making, by the judicious combination of logwood, aloes, strychnine, and other harmless drugs of that nature, with the necessary coloring matters, all kinds of liquors, from the rare and costly wines of France and Spain, to the cheap whisky which kills its victims at forty rods.

From that time Slocum considered his fortune made. True, people began to wonder how it was, that he could make so much liquor, and that of every description, out of so little grain, but the sworn distiller, and the dark cellar faithfully kept their secret, and none knew of the wonderful transformations going on there.

Another thing they noticed was, that Slocum's liquor had a strange effect upon anyone who drank any quantity of it. It not only made them drunk, but it made them demons. They would become raving maniacs; while several who had drank to excess, had died with all the indications of poisoning. However, the coroner was a member of the whisky party, and did not feel justified in putting the county to the expense of an inquest over a poor, drunken pauper, so they were buried without, and the grave, like the dark cellar, faithfully kept its secret, and the work of death went on.

Having, during this explanation, given Squire Slocum time to rest himself and throw off the superabundance of carbon, with which his body is charged, he is ready for business.

"Are you alone," he first asked, glancing cautiously around the room.

"Quite alone, Squire," replied the Hon. Hezekiah; "what is up now? Anybody been crossing your path?"

"Well, no, —or, at least, not exactly; but I have rather an important business that I want attended to, and you know I always employ you, and you have never yet failed," he added with a knowing look, which was easily understood by the wily lawyer.

"At your service, Squire."

"You know that drunken lawyer, Hank Wardsworth, who was in here to execute some papers a while ago?"

"Know him? I think I have reason to know him."

"Yes, yes, I remember now, when he used to keep sober he was considered more than your match;" and the Squire gave a coarse laugh which ended in a wheeze and a cough.

"I don't care for that so much, but confound the rascal, had it not been for his drunken twaddle, I would have received the nomination for the legislature. I have sworn to get even with him yet; though for that matter, if he keeps on as he is going now, he will soon spare me that trouble, or I am much mistaken in the character of Solomon Slocum's whisky."

Somehow the Squire didn't seem to relish this remark of Simkins, but allowing it to pass, he continued:

"That is just what I came to see you about.

You know his residence up on Maple stree."

"Yes, I have often admired that place, wouldn't mind owning it myself. Bought it with money left him by his dead father, I understand."

"So I am told. How much do you think the property worth?"

"Well from ten to twelve thousand, I should judge."

"I think so. It is all going to rack, and ought to be owned by someone who will keep it in repair, and not allow it to be a disgrace to the avenue."

"Oh! I understand. You think it would make a very nice residence for the family of Solomon Slocum, Esq."

"Well, you can put it in that way. You remember I already hold a mortgage on it of three thousand dollars."

"Yes, I know I drew and executed a mortgage for that amount; but for the life of me, Slocum, I can't understand how he ever came to be indebted to you in that amount. However, you are sure enough of the property; he will never be able to redeem the mortgage."

"True enough, but perhaps some other man may have his eye upon it, and admire it as much as I do. In that case, if I were to sell it under this mortgage, I might have to pay more for it than I care to."

"How do you propose to manage it then?"

"I propose to increase the mortgage. Or, what is the same thing, get another one on the same property. Listen; and I will explain;" and the eyes of Slocum turned away from the steady gaze of the man whom he knew to be as big a rogue as himself. "You see Wardsworth has become sadly addicted to the vice of gambling. In fact, the greater part of what he owes me now is for money spent at the gaming table. The whole property is sure to go that way, and I may, as well have it as for the keeper of some low groggery to get it."

"I understand that well enough," replied the lawyer, "but how do you propose to get it? That is what I fail to comprehend."

"That is just what I am coming at," and Slocum turned his gaze still further from that of the lawyer. "You know Colonel Bradshaw?"

"Bradshaw the gambler? Yes, but what of him?"

"Our plan is simply this: Bradshaw has offered, for five hundred dollars, to play against Wardsworth. We will get Hank about half drunk, and in that condition he always plays so long as he can raise a dollar; though when he is sober you can't get him to touch a card. My plan, therefore, is to meet, we three, in some quiet place, say your office. Let Bradshaw and Wardsworth begin to play. Of course Hank will lose. I will agree to stand security for all the money he wants to bet, taking a second mortgage on his place. We can let it run as long as we like, I becoming responsible to Bradshaw for whatever he wins. When the amount has reached four or five thousand dollars, you can draw the mortgage and we will get Wardsworth to sign it. As I said, if the plan is successful, Bradshaw's fee is to be five hundred dollars, and I don't mind making yours the same."

For a moment the ex-legislator was shocked. He had seen roguery in every form, had been familiar with many of the scoundrels and blacklegs in the country, but the cool, deliberate planning of so terrible a crime. so hellish a scheme to rob an unfortunate victim of his home, and that of his wife and child, he never yet had seen. Hardened as he was himself, this proposition of Slocum's revealed a purpose so deadly that, for a moment, he could hardly believe the evidence of his senses. For an instant his lost manhood seemed determined to reassert itself, and move him to kick the scoundrel out doors. But he remembered that he too, was in Slocum's power; besides, the fee of five hundred dollars was very tempting. Only for a moment was his better nature able to continue the struggle. Avarice and fear combined and conquered; and turning to Slocum, he answered:

"All right, Slocum? I am ready to do my part in the infamous transaction, but when the gentleman from the lower regions comes, looking for the most infamous scoundrel on earth, I shall direct him to the residence of Solomon Slocum, Esq."

Even so, men think to wash their hands of the very sin they commit.

This home thrust made Slocum wince. He turned, if possible, still redder in the face than before; but gathering boldness from success, he retorted:

"You needn't think to play Pontius Pilate in that manner, Simpkins. Perhaps I know another gentleman who wont come far behind in that race, if he does write Hon. before his name.

But don't let us quarrel over the matter. You say you will consent to my proposal, so let us arrange particulars. Let me see, this is Tuesday. Suppose you see Wardsworth, and get on the good side of him, and make an appointment to meet me here some evening next week. You can adopt your own plan to get him here, and when you have made the appointment, let me know, and I will arrange the rest."

And with a sort of demoniac smile, Slocum took his cane and departed.*

*Does the reader regard this as an impossible picture? We assure him that such a case was known to the author, in which a personal friend was a victim. It but serves to illustrate the terrible power for evil of our nation's horrible curse—the liquor traffic; the right hand of the gambler —the weapon of the vicious in their warfare against virtue.

CHAPTER V.

THE VICTIM.

Morning dawned bright and beautiful at the home of the Wardsworth's. The glad sunshine streamed down, enveloping the earth in floods of golden light, but it brought no sunshine to the weary hearts within. The birds poured forth their sweetest melodies, but they awakened no echoing response from the sad inmates. In the chamber, morn looked down on the weary, care-worn watcher, worn out with sorrow's vigil, and "sick with a heart-breaking sadness," and, in the parlor, on the once proud and happy husband, still fast locked in the slumbers of the inebriate. The deep, dark flush that rested on his face, when he returned, had given place to a more natural hue. The hair had fallen back from his forehead, revealing a brow and face, of surpassing beauty, and one that once seen is not easily forgotten. In spite of his degredation, the stamp of intellectual greatness and nobility yet remained. As we stand and look at him lying there, with all that greatness a mass of ruins, his manhood shorn of its strength, the fire of his genius quenched,—and when we re-

member what he was, and all he gave promise
yet to become, and then remember that he is but
the representative of a vast army of *seventy
thousand* such victims, which, in christian
America, are being annually crushed beneath
the remorseless hoofs of the rum traffic, we cannot refrain from uttering the direst curses
against the foul monster. Oh! citizens of our
glorious Republic, to you we turn, and implore
you to listen to the agonizing cries that come
from those seventy thousand. You who hold
in your hand that most sacred of all trusts, the
ballot of an American voter, why will you permit this wholesale slaughter of humanity's
noblest specimens? Why will you let so foul a
tyrant rule over this nation of free men and
free women? Why will you permit so foul a
pestilence to depopulate our shores to the extent of seventy thousand a year, when you hold
in your hands the power to prevent it? Why
do you give your consent and approval to the
desolation of seventy thousand homes? Why
will you not interpose to prevent the breaking
of the hearts of seventy thousand mothers, wives
and children, some of whom may yet be of your
own flesh and blood. Will not the blood of
those victims be required at your hands? Can
you wash your hands and truthfully say, "I am
innocent," knowing that you possess the *power*
to prevent this, and yet refuse to exercise that
power? Citizens of America, let your voice be

heard. Go to the suffering, heart-broken inmates of those seventy thousand homes and tell
them to hope. Tell them that their cry has at
last reached the ear of the Nation, and it will
come to their deliverance. Go! Do this! and
the blessings of high heaven will attend you.

Mrs. Wardsworth was the first to awaken on
that morning of sorrow, and softly rising, so as
not to disturb little Harry, she descended to
the parlor. Her husband was still sleeping,
and entering softly, she knelt down at the head
of the sofa, and, as she looked into his face and
caressed the dark locks into which there had
not yet entered a single gray hair, remembering
the days when he stood up in the nobility of a
truer, better manhood, a great flood of tenderness and love swept over her soul, and she
could not resist the impulse to stoop down and
imprint upon that brow an impassioned kiss.
This act awakened him. Just for a moment a
glad smile played upon his countenance, then
the memory of all his degradation came back
upon him, and he could no longer look up into
the pale tearful face of his injured wife, but
turning his face to the wall, he wept such tears
as are only wrung from a heart filled with a
hopeless despair.

Tenderly the loving wife stole her arm under
his neck, and drawing his head until it rested
upon her bosom, she mingled her tears with
his. And angels paused in their heavenward

flight, and looking down on that scene of love and devotion, caught up the whisperings of that prayer of faith, and carrying them all up, laid them down before the throne of the Eternal, and they were placed on record in the book of God's remembrance, and over against them was written, "The fervent, effectual prayers of the righteous availeth much."

For some moments they remained thus, neither speaking, till, at last, the silence was broken by the husband.

"It is no use, Belle, I know how unworthy I am of your devotion. What a sad failure I have made of life, but all my good resolutions are like ropes of sand before the power of the tempter. The demon of drink has bound me hand and foot, and there is nothing left but for you to let me go. I am only dragging you down lower and lower. Oh, God! if I alone could suffer; but that I should make those I love the victims of my degradation. Oh, to stand on the brink of an awful precipice and know that I am doomed to go over. To see the deep, dark pit before me, and no power to avoid it. To know that all the dearest treasures of my life are destined to be involved in the general ruin, and yet compelled to move helplessly on to my doom. Oh! I wish I had never been born;" and the strong man shook with the very intensity of emotion.

"Oh my dear husband, do not talk so. Have

I not vowed before God to love and cherish you
till death do us part? True, my heart sometimes almost breaks with the intensity of my
grief; but it is for you and little Harry. Not
for myself do I grieve. But oh, my Harry, the
husband of my joy, will you not try once more
to conquer your deadly foe? Oh, let my love
plead, not for myself, but for you, the dearest
and most loved of all the treasures God ever
gave me. By the memory of those happy days,
all too quickly fled, for the sake of future joys
which may even yet be ours, promise me that
you will make one more effort."

"Alas, Belle! it seems worse than useless to
promise. Have I not promised time and again,
only to deceive your hopes? What prospect is
there for a man like me, when on every street
corner there stands a saloon? When I cannot
walk down the street without inhaling the
fumes of liquor, which arouses all the powers
of this morbid, craving appetite? A thousand
temptations are around me on every side. For a
poor wretch like me there is no hope but to
drift with the current until I reach the cataract
and then plunge beneath the dark waters.
But for your sake, Belle, my injured wife, and
for little Harry's I will promise; I will make
one more effort. Perhaps I may yet recover
myself; and oh, my dear wife, whatever the result of this struggle may be, do believe me, I
want to conquer, I want to be free."

The breakfast bell here rang, and going to his own room, Wardsworth made a hasty toilet and descended to the dining-room. His wife had not yet entered; and he waited a few moments. She soon came, wearing her old cheerful smile, so much so that her husband wondered. Ah! had he but followed her as she went into the council chamber of her God, had he heard her as she plead the Divine promises, had he seen the look of holy faith and trust, as the Spirit came down and sealed the witness upon her heart, the secret of her cheerfulness would have been explained.

The days passed on and lengthened into weeks, and still Harry Wardsworth kept his promise. He attended to whatever business he had, which was but little, it is true, and seemed in part, to be himself once more. But a cloud was over him. He possessed but little of his old cheerfulness and vitality. He seemed to perform his duties in a sort of mechanical way, but it was evident he had but very little heart in his work. Still he kept sober, and this, to his wife, was a source of untold joy. Oh! how earnestly she labored, how faithfully she watched, and sought by every means in her power, to lift the shadow from his heart. She walked with him to the gate, met him there on his return, had his dressing gown and slippers ready for him, and in every possible way strove to make his home so attractive that he would have no desire to leave it. She sang the old songs he used to love, watching his every mood, and adapting everything to his tastes and wishes. And her faith grew stronger and her hopes brighter as she witnessed his strong determination to conquer and break the chain that bound him. As the weeks passed, and she saw his old smile come back to him again, and as his walk grew quicker and more vigorous, she felt that the blessing for which she had so long prayed had indeed come.

His friends, too, began to rally around him. The white haired old pastor, under whose ministry he had long sat, knelt in his family circle and prayed with a fervency that was born of hope. His friend, Dr. Thornton, congratulated him on his improved appearance. Altogether, there was a brighter prospect of ultimate triumph than for long months before.

This was the condition of things when, one day, as Wardsworth was walking down street, he was met and accosted by the Hon. Hezekiah Simkins.

"Why, how are you, Wardsworth," exclaimed the lawyer, "I am truly glad to see you looking so well. You look like a new man."

Wardsworth's first impulse was to give him a short answer and pass on; but it was never in his nature to be rude, so he paused and entered into a short conversation.

"By the way, Wardsworth," said Simkins, "I

have been looking for some one to take two or
three cases I have, as I have to be gone for a
week or two, and you are just the man I want.
I shall be pleased to put them in your hands.
They are important cases, and I don't know of
any one I would as soon trust them with as
yourself. What do you say?"

"I shall be glad to take them, Simkins, and
shall feel grateful to you as well. To tell the
truth, business has been very dull with me
lately, and I need all the legitimate work I
can get"—with a slight accent on the word
legitimate.

. "Let me see," said Simkins, "I shall be from
home to-morrow and next day. If you will call
at my office next day evening, I will explain
the cases to you. I have no doubt but that
you will be successful and the fee will be
liberal."

"I know of nothing to prevent me from coming," replied Wardsworth, though, truth to tell,
he felt ill at ease in the presence of the wily
lawyer. Thus, however, the appointment was
made, and the two men separated; the one to
enter the purer atmosphere of his home, and
the other to report to Slocum the success of his
plan. That gentleman(?) was delighted with
the prospect, and instantly started in quest of
his friend, Colonel Bradshaw, arranged for him
to drop into Simpkins' office about 9 P. M. the
next evening but one. Thus the trap was laid,

and the trio of *honorable* gentlemen only awaited the presence of their victim to spring it.

"I shall not be at home this evening quite as early as usual, my dear," remarked Wardsworth to his wife, the next evening at tea. "I have promised to call at Simkins' office. He has a few important cases he wishes me to take, as he is going away for a short time."

The countenance of Mrs. Wardsworth fell. A sad foreboding seized her heart. She remembered, all too vividly, other evenings when he had gone out, expecting to return shortly, and the coils were thrown around him, and she dared not think of what the result might be again. Still she nerved herself and resolved to hope for the best. She could not harbor the thought of even a possibility of her short heaven of happiness being invaded by the dark form of sorrow. She assisted in changing dressing gown for coat, she walked with him down to the front gate, and there, with the bright moon beams as witnesses, she wound her arms around his neck and sent him away with a wife's pure kiss upon his cheek, even though there were fear and trembling in her heart.

Wardsworth was surprised, on reaching Simkin's office, to find there no less a personage than Solomon Slocum; but as that gentleman soon rose to take his departure, he presumed it was merely accidental. Had he but *known* the dark, secret purposes of those two men! but he did not.

"Call in about an hour Squire," said Simkins, "and I will be through with Mr. Wardsworth, and will finish your business."

The reader is, no doubt, by this time fully aware that it was no part of Simkins' plan to put any cases into the hands of Wardsworth. On the contrary, the latter was there in accordance with the deep laid plot for his ruin. Nor will he be surprised when he learns that the very first thing Simkins did, was to bring out and set on his desk a bottle of what he called "pure old French wine," but which was nothing more than some of Slocum's poison.

Of all the arts and wiles Simkins made use of to induce Wardsworth to drink, the reader need not be told. Has he, too, not seen them practiced? Are they not as common as the gin palaces of our country? Are not the victims of those wiles continually reeling along our streets? Are they not crouching and hiding from the curses and blows of those whom those wiles have robbed of their manhood and their reason? Are they not uttering the "low, sad wail of anguish" over the dishonored graves of husbands, sons, brothers and fathers? Ah! but too sadly familiar are our readers with those experiences, or spectacles, to require any explanation of them from our pen. Suffice it therefore, to say, before the cunning and crafty wiles of the deceitful lawyer, the good resolutions of Wardsworth proved too feeble. Home with all its endearments, his wife with her smiles and songs and loving counsels, his babe with its prattle and childish glee, health, wealth, honor, all the mighty barriers raised by virtue, gave way before the fierce onslaught of the tempter, and again the demon had his coils around his victim. He at last yielded under a sacred promise of Simkins, that he should be asked to take but one glass. But one glass taken, the appetite was aroused, the lion was unchained, and from that moment the villain's task was easy. The result was, that when Slocum, who by the way had "accidently" run across Bradshaw, during his absence, returned, he found Wardsworth in the very condition he desired. Nothing was more plausible than for Slocum to express surprise at finding Wardsworth still there; but, as there were four of them, a game of cards, "merely for pleasure you know, would be just the thing." The result can be imagined.

Does the reader wonder, does he express surprise, that all this could be accomplished for the ruin of Wardsworth? Does he ask, how could he be so unwise, so easily overcome? Why did he not refuse to yield, and tearing away from those who compassed his ruin, return at once to the safe and sacred refuge of his home? True, reader, this would have been the wise and safe course. But do you ask why he did not do it? Then you know nothing of the power of an inebriate's appetite. Go stand on the shore of the ocean, whose billows have reached the mountain surge, and bid them cease their rolling. Go stand amid the deafening roar of the mighty Niagara, and bid the pouring cataract turn back upon itself. Go bid defiance to the thunder, and command the lightning to cease its flashing. Turn back the hurricane and the tempest. Bid the avalanche stand still, midway down the mountain side. Go, and when you have accomplished all these, undertake to control the demon appetite for strong drink when once it is aroused in the breast of its victim.

What wonder then, with all this odds against him, that Wardsworth fell? Fell as he had fallen before. Lower and lower, deeper and deeper in the pit of hopeless ruin. Alas for Wardsworth! Alas for his wife and child! Alas for the home that shelters them! Where is the angel that watches over him? Justice, where is thy sword? Love and sympathy, whither have ye fled? Pity, hast thou left the human breast? Is there no strong arm that may be outstretched to save?

By midnight, Harry Wardsworth was not only shorn of his manhood, but bereft of his reason and robbed of his home. He played with the recklessness of a maniac. Bradshaw had only to name the amount and Wardsworth immediately covered it, on the promise of Slocum that he would see it paid. At one o'clock Bradshaw had won from him $3,500. Then was the time for the execution of the most diabolical part of their plan. At this point Slocum paused and refused to stand security for Wardsworth's losses. He held that it was a debt of honor, and Wardsworth ought to secure it. But if he would give him a second mortgage on his place he would make it $4,000, and stand good for another $500. To this the victim consented. In an incredible short time, so short, indeed, as to afford almost positive evidence that he had it prepared beforehand, Simkins produced the mortgage. Here, however, the victim wavered. Through his maddened brain there seemed to glimmer a thought of what he was doing, and he hesitated. Another glass of Slocum's wine, and then the hellish deed was done. As best it could, the trembling hand affixed the *signature*, and the beautiful house of Harry Wardsworth passed, to all intents and purposes, into the hands of Solomon Slocum. One game more, and the last $500 for which Slocum stood security was lost, and Wardsworth and his family were paupers.

Then out into the darkness. Into the deep, silent night, where the stars looked down with pitying eyes. To his home? No, not there. Not where his wife sat at the window, watching and waiting for his return. Not where his

babe nestled in his crib and waited so long for
papa's good night kiss. Not where the peace
and warmth and safety of home love had been
wont to throw around him their protecting
shield. Not where the joyous song even yet
waited, trembling on the lips, and only needed
the light of his manhood's presence, to break
forth in tones of delight. No, not there. He
had gone out with his manhood upon him. He
had left his home in the strength of his reason,
and with a wife's pure kiss upon his cheek.
Now what was he? A being to be despised
and shunned. No, he could not go home. He
could not meet the tender, tearful eyes of the
wife whom he still loved, but whom he had so
deeply wronged. These were the thoughts
that, in a confused manner, passed through his
mind as he wandered on in the darkness. On
through the deserted streets, where no light
gleamed upon his path. Out where the trees
lifted up their imploring arms, where the flowers bloomed by the wayside, and the apple
blossoms gave forth their joyous fragrance,
as if they fain would compensate for man's cruelty. On, on, until his weary feet refused to
do his bidding, and his now poisoned body sank
from sheer exhaustion, and he fell by the wayside, unconscious alike of his degradation and
his doom. Still the stars looked down in solemn pity. Night, the silent witness of all
his wrongs, gently enwrapped the sleeping form

in her sable robes, and nature wept a million drops of dew at the sad spectacle of "man's inhumanity to man."

Slocum's plan had succeeded beyond his most sanguine expectations. It was just as he wanted it. Should the validity of the mortgage be questioned, were there not three respectable gentlemen who could give testimony that all was fair and square? What mattered it, though he had committed robbery most cool and cowardly. Though perjury the foulest lay deep upon his soul? Had he not secured what his avarice coveted, the home of Harry Wardsworth?

Slowly passed the hours of night, and still the patient, weary wife continued her vigil. As the night advanced and her husband came not, hope gave place to fear and anxiety. But when "the clock in the tower struck two," and still no signs of his coming, a dull weight of sorrow settled upon her breast. Reason and a too sad experience alike bore testimony that there could be but one cause for his absence. The buoyancy of hope gave place to the darkness of despair.

Would, dear reader, that this were an imaginary, or even a solitary picture; but it is not. Over all this otherwise free and happy land, there are thousands of such sad, weary vigils. A mother watches for her boy, whose feet have been turned in the way of darkness. A wife watches for the husband, who, overcome by an

appetite, *formed in accordance with law,* lies
helpless in the grasp of his enemy. Alas for
the weary, helpless watchers, when the power
of that law, which should be the refuge of the
weak and defenseless, is in league with the hosts
of rum.

Slowly and sadly passed the hours of night.
The grey dawn, harbinger of the coming day,
stole up from the far east. The bright beams
of the morning streamed down on valley and
hill. The flowers opened their petals to wel-
come the glad sunshine, the birds came forth
from their quiet resting place, where nature's
hand had built their shelter, and awoke the
earth with their morning song. The bells rang
out the morning call, and the mechanic went
forth to his toil. The city awoke to new life,
and again was heard the busy hum of industry,
but Harry Wardsworth came not. His wife,
filled with apprehension and alarm, called to
her aid a few chosen friends, who undertook to
search for him.

Simkins was seen, who stated that he left his
office about ten in the evening, and that so far
as he could judge he was sober. At last a man
was seen who said he had found a person bearing his description by the roadside, and had
brought him to the city, leaving him at a certain corner; and that he appeared to be either
sick or intoxicated. Then began the search in
earnest. Down into the basement saloons,

where men hide away from the gaze of the multitude, that they may do evil. Searching over the records of the police station, in the gin palaces of the "respectable" where the liquid poison and death is held in bottles radiant with bands of silver and gold. All day the search continued. To each inquiry, every saloon-keeper answered they had not seen him.

"Is it Harry Wardsworth you are looking for?" asked a poor, half drunken man, as two of his friends passed out of one of the saloons.

"Yes. Can you tell us anything about him?"

"I reckon I can, only you must not go back on me if I tell you."

"You need not fear," said Dr. Thornton, "no harm shall come to you in the least, so long as you are not implicated in any way."

"Well, then look about Walt Pitman's saloon and you will find him."

"But we have just been there, and Mr. Pitman says he is not there and has not been there."

"Did you look for yourselves? Not in the bar room, I mean, but out around?"

"No, we did not. But he can't be stowed away there, can he?"

"I reckon that is just what they does with 'em, sir, that is the respectable ones. They don't let 'em stay in the saloon when they get so awful drunk; they stows 'em away. Leastwise, you go to Pitman's and look around and you'll find him;" and with a motion of the hand toward Pitman's saloon, he was gone.

"Possibly he may be right, after all,". said Dr. Thornton; "let us go back to Pitman's and look around. There is no trusting the word of those fellows."

So back to Pitman's they went, and began a thorough search of the premises, so far as they were able, without subjecting themselves to a charge of trespass. At last they found him. But where, reader, do you think he was found? In an old out-house, among boxes and barrels, lying on a bundle of hay in a state of perfect unconsciousness.*

And Walter Pitman, it was said, kept the most respectable saloon in the city; and perhaps he did. His place was the resort of all the better class of drinkers. His *place of business*, licensed by law, you know, was one of the most nicely fitted and furnished in the city. Mirrors hung on the walls, costly decanters contained the sparkling wines, and, in short, the place was so respectable that the proprietor, rather than suffer the disgrace of having Wardsworth found on his premises drunk, after robbing him of his money and his reason, prefered to stow him away in an out-house and then lie about his being there. Moreover, Pitman knew Wardsworth as well as he knew his

---

*A true incident, in which the author assisted in the search.

brother. He knew his friends were anxiously searching for him. He knew that he had received favors from Harry Wardsworth without number, yet with all this, Pitman was too respectable to do him a kindness, and send him home. Has not the reader seen the same scene enacted time and again? Its counterpart may be found in almost every town and city in the land. Such is the cruelty of rum.

We say that Harry Wardsworth was found, but oh how changed! What a terrible wreck the twenty-four hours had made. Could that ghastly, besotted looking being be the noble looking husband and father, who went out but yesterday, with the glad laugh of his child still ringing in his ears, and a wife's pure kiss still warm upon his cheek?

They carried him to his home. Alas! his no longer; and there, through the long hours of the night, kind friends watched him in his long bitter struggle with imaginary demons, and tried to comfort his grief-stricken wife.

The struggle continued even down to the very doors of death; but at last nature triumphed, and slowly rallying, he drifted back again to life. But his hopes seemed crushed and his powers of resistance gone. A few feeble efforts were made, but they accomplished nothing. He seemed to have passed the turning point, beyond which scarcely dawns a ray of hope. To be tempted was to yield, and soon it became a

common saying, "Poor Wardsworth is drunk
again." The wife's cup of misery seemed full.

CHAPTER VI.

THE COMFORTER.

The family of Rev. Chas. Bradley had risen
from breakfast, and the pastor had retired to
his study to finish his Sunday morning's ser-
mon, when the servant returned from the post-
office and handed Mrs. Bradley a letter addressed to herself. It was postmarked "Cedarville," and the address was in the hand-writing
of her sister, Belle. Something in the address
seemed strange, and filled her with apprehension and fear. A strange foreboding seized
her, and it was some moments before she could
open the letter. The writing was evidently
her sister's but it had the appearance of having
been the work of a trembling hand. She broke
the seal, and after reading the letter twice
over, sat some moments in thoughtful meditation. Mr. Bradley had reached one of the most
interesting portions of his discourse, when the
study door opened and his wife entered.

"Can you spare me from home for a few
weeks, husband," she asked.

Looking at her a moment, in some surprise,
he answered pleasantly:

"I presume I can, my dear, if you wish. Where do you want to go?"

For answer, his wife placed in his hand, her sister's letter. He took it and read as follows:

CEDARVILLE, June —, 18—.

Dear Sister Kate:—You remember when on that bright May morning, now five years ago, I stood up, and in the glad joyousness of my girlhood, took upon me the solemn vows of wife. And you remember when you, my dearest friend, while rejoicing with me in my happiness, bade me remember that life was not all sunshine, I even laughed at the thought, that to me could ever come sorrow.

You know not, dear sister, how sadly I have learned the bitter lesson. Hitherto I have tried to write cheerfully, for I have hoped for the best; but now all hope seems gone and my heart is breaking with the fullness of its grief.

You remember on the morning of my marriage, you referred to Harry's habit of drinking wine; and said that was the only dark cloud you could discern on the horizon of my life. I could not then believe there could be the slightest danger; but, oh! how bitterly I have been compelled to mourn my mistake. Slowly, but surely, the serpent has wound his deadly coils around my dear husband until, all helpless he lies in the grasp of his foe. Oh! dear sister, what shall I do? My pen refuses to write the sad words expressive of my sufferings.

Is it too much to ask of you, dear sister, to come to me. for a short time! I need you, oh, so much! Do not, when you write home, tell the dear ones there the story of my trials. It would almost kill them. I am glad they are all far enough away not to hear it. May God bless them, and make their life flow smoothly on, whatever becomes of me.

Write me, and if you can come, please do so without delay. Your loving sister,

BELLE WARDSWORTH.

Mr. Bradley read the letter over carefully, and after a few moments thought, said:

"It does seem like a call of duty. I think you had better go and carry all the comfort you can. Poor girl, if that is the state of affairs she is indeed in want of all the sympathy it is possible to impart. When can you be ready to start?"

"This is Thursday," answered his wife, "not before Monday, I think. I have some work I must do for the children first. I can finish that this week, and be ready to start Monday."

"Very well. You had better get ready to go on that day—dropping her a note to that effect by to-day's mail. And one word more, Kate, I fear you will find matters worse than we expect. Should they have reached a crisis, don't fail to give Belle the warmest assurance of a place in our home and our hearts. Poor girl, to think that one so pure and so loving should know the sad pangs of a drunkard's wife."

"Thank you, my dear husband, it is what I might have expected from one so noble;" and the proud wife imprinted a fervent kiss upon his cheek.

The balance of the week all was hurry and bustle at the parsonage. Mrs. Bradley had much to do before she could leave her own little family comfortable, and yet she often found herself pausing in the midst of her work, to picture the sad, lone sister in the far away western home. Time dragged heavily, although her hands were so busy; and for the first time in all her married years, she was glad when the hour arrived that was to see her borne away from the home of her household treasures.

As already intimated, Mrs. Bradley was the senior of her sister Belle, by two years. Three years before the opening of our story, she had married the Rev. Chas. Bradley, the beloved pastor of a large and prosperous congregation in a city but a few miles from the home of her parents in the State of New York. Hitherto, Mrs. Wardsworth had taken the greatest care to conceal her trouble, not once referring to it in her letters, but writing with as hopeful a spirit as possible. But the loving sister had become satisfied that it was not all sunshine with her. A tone of pensive sadness ran through all her letters and once she detected what she believed to be a tear stain. She was not, therefore, unprepared to hear of the sad state of affairs which Belle's letter revealed.

Wednesday evening brought her to her destination. Mrs. Wardsworth had not yet, from some cause, received the note advising her of her coming, and was therefore not fully prepared to receive her. She had just tucked little Harry away in his crib, and had sat down to her work, when a carriage halted at the gate and a lady alighted. Instantly she knew it was her sister Kate. Had she had time to get control of her feelings, she would have been more composed; but as it was, she had only strength to totter to the door, when she fell into the arms of her sister. All the long pent-up feelings of the soul burst instantly forth, and it was with the greatest difficulty that Mrs. Bradley could get her into the room and keep her from fainting. She sat her down upon the sofa, and took her head upon her breast, just as she used to in those old days, when together they nestled in the dear old home. The poor, aching heart had at length found a refuge. No words were yet spoken, but the elder sister was glad to see that the younger had found relief in tears. For herself, she could only press the dear form closer to her breast and let her weep. Presently she became calmer, and raising her tear-stained face, she imprinted one long impassioned kiss, that revealed at once her soul's deep love and all the long story of her heart's bitter sorrow.

"I am so glad to see you, sister, but I wish I had known you were coming so soon."

"Did you not get my letter informing you of my visit? I received yours on Thursday and wrote immediately that I would start on Monday. I would have telegraphed, but I supposed you would surely get the letter."

"Never mind, it is all right now," and again she wound her arms around the sister's neck and laid her head on her bosom, just as a child who feels that there alone it is safe.

As she thus lay, with her sad face upturned to her sister's, for a moment Mrs. Bradley could not suppress the bitter thoughts that came unbidden to her heart. Oh! what a sad wreck these five years had made of that once light-hearted and happy girl. Could that pale-faced woman, with those shrunken cheeks and those hollow eyes, be the glad, merry-hearted sister Belle of only five years ago? Could this be the same being who proudly stood up and took upon her, her wifely vows, and then went so joyously out from the shelter of the home roof? Alas! it is not Time's destroying hand that has early robbed this flower of its bloom. It is not the wasting touch of disease that has robbed the eye of its lustre and the cheek of its rose. "An enemy hath done this! "A foe more deadly cruel than disease and death hath stolen into

this dear treasure house and left his desolating
track; and as she thought of all that innocent
being had suffered, as she recognized that all
this was but a system of legalized murder, the
more cruel because it killed so slowly, she felt
like invoking Heaven's direst vengeance on the
liquor traffic and all concerned therein. But
better thoughts ere long prevailed. A feeling
of yearning tenderness came over her, and her
heart went out in pitying prayer, not only for
the helpless suffering wife, but for the wander-
ing, erring husband as well.

Very carefully and tenderly, little by little,
the wise and thoughtful Mrs. Bradley drew out
the story of her sister's wrongs, and learned
that her husband's worst fears were more than
realized. Everything was gone. Even some
of their best furniture had been sold to supply
them with the necessaries of life. "The saddest part of it all is," said Mrs. Wardsworth,
after they had talked a long while, "we have
to leave this once beautiful home. Though, as
to that, it has become to me more like a prison
than a home."

"Why, how is that?" asked Mrs. Bradley,
"has Harry become so deeply involved?"

At this question the wife buried her face in
her hands and again gave way to a fit of weeping. When she again controlled herself and
looked up, there was a blush on her cheeks
that told but too plainly how deeply she felt

her husband's degradation which she was forced to reveal.

"I cannot tell how it is, but I awfully fear, that to the vice of drinking, Harry has added that of gambling. A man by the name of Slocum, living in the city, and who owns a large distillery, says he holds a mortgage on it for seven thousand dollars. The neighbors say it is worth ten thousand, but it is so fast going to decay that it wont be worth the mortgage much longer. I cannot understand how ever Harry got in debt to him so much. I have spoken to him of it once or twice, but I see it affects him so badly that I have ceased to mention it. Of one thing I am certain, Harry never had that much money from him, or I would have had some of it. I fully believe my husband has been robbed, but we are helpless and can do nothing but submit,"

"What does this man Slocum propose to do? Does he want to take the place himself?"

"Yes. He was here a few days ago, and said that the place was so fast going to the bad that it would not be security for the amount much longer. That he hated to foreclose the mortgage, for if he did, the balance would be all eaten up with costs; but if I and Mr. Wardsworth would consent to give up the place without the necessity of foreclosure, he would give us five hundred dollars. Harry was not at home, and I have not yet spoken to him about it. I suppose, however, it is the best we can do."

"Where is Harry, now?" presently asked Mrs. Bradley.

At this question a look of terrible suffering came into the face of Mrs. Wardsworth, but she controlled herself and replied:

"I have not seen him since yesterday morning. He has got so now that he don't come home when he is drinking so very hard, but stays at the saloon until his money is all gone."

"Well, Belle, I have a message from my husband, and I will deliver it now. It is that if at any time you may feel it necessary to sever the connection with your husband, our home and our hearts are open to receive you,"—and Mrs. Bradley again folded the sorrowful woman to her breast.

Mrs. Wardsworth drew herself up and something like the old pride came back, and a bright spot burned on her cheeks as she answered:

"It was not for that you came was it Kate? For if it was, I may as well say to you now, once for all, that when I wedded Harry Wardsworth, I wedded him for life, and *never* till death doth us part will I forsake him. Besides, my hopes are not all dead yet,"—and a sad, sweet smile stole over her face. "You remember, Kate, the refuge of which we learned in our dear old home. I have never yet forgotten the pathway to a throne of grace, and when all else has failed, that has supported me still."

"Heaven bless you for those noble words, dear Belle. And now in answer to your question. No, it was not for that I came. I am thankful, dear sister, that your love and faith have survived this trying ordeal. God grant that they may yet be victorious. But if worst comes to worst, know where you may find a safe shelter and as much of joy as may be. But now it is long past midnight, and you have not yet shown me this wonderful little Harry about which you have so often written me." At the mention of his name the mother's eye brightened and something like a glad smile played on her face as she led the way to an adjoining room, and holding the lamp in one hand, stooped down and pressed a warm kiss upon the soft cheek, an example that was followed by the elder sister. The intrusion disturbed the slumbering boy, and turning uneasily in his crib, murmured the name— "papa." "Somehow, Kate," remarked Belle, "I cannot help but believe that in some way God will use our boy as a means of reclaiming my husband. He loves me just as dearly as he ever did, but he fairly worships little Harry. Oh if he had only power to crush his foe, but I confess that sometimes my hope grows weak. And yet I find that in spite of all, my faith still clings more and more to the belief that the boy will yet be the saviour of the man."

"God grant that it may be so, and in his own good time and manner," replied her sister, "and now let us have prayer and retire."

Together they knelt, side by side, just as they had done in those long gone happy days of girlhood, and poured their supplications into the ear of their loving Father. Oh how strongly and fervently did the wife plead for her erring husband. Like the patriarch of old, she clung to the arm of God, and refused to let him go until she obtained the blessing. And her prayer fell upon the ear of him who never yet hath said, "Seek ye my face in vain." The messenger of peace came down, and sealed the spirit's witness upon her heart; the recording angel wrote her supplication in Heaven's register, and over against her prayer was written the Divine assurance, "They shall call upon me in the day of trouble and I will deliver them."

CHAPTER VII.

THE SHADOWS DEEPEN.

When Harry Wardsworth first began to absent himself from home, during his seasons of dissipation, his wife would use every effort to find him and induce him to return. For a time she was in this successful, but for a while back failing in her efforts, she had given up the practice, finding that it only served to irritate him, besides subjecting herself to a great deal of shame and suffering. On the morning following her sister's arrival, however, finding he had not returned, a strange foreboding seized her. There came to her a presentiment of impending danger, which she found it impossible to throw off. She strove to cast it aside, but all in vain. She had made the fire—for a long time she had done all the work about the house—and had set about preparing breakfast, when the door bell rang, and a stranger handed her a note, saying it was from her husband, and immediately departed. For a moment she was so overcome that she found it impossible to break the seal. Collecting herself, she opened the note, and read as follows. She recognized her husband's writing, although it was almost unintelligible.   It said:

"*My Injured Wife:*—The end has at last come, and I am in prison.   Last night, in a fit of in-toxication I struck a man and so injured him that it is feared he will die.   Before God, my dear wife, I have not the slightest knowledge of what transpired.   Perhaps it is better so, on-ly for you and little Harry.   May God pity you and forgive me."

On reading the note, Mrs. Wardsworth im-mediatly called her sister, and then hastened her preparations for breakfast, intending as soon as it was over, to go in search of her hus-band.   She had nearly finished preparing the meal, when a neighbor called—one of those sympathizing kind, who think the deeper they can probe the wound in a human heart, the greater kindness they do them—and handed her a morning paper, saying, "Here, Mrs. Wards-worth, is something about your husband, I thought it would be a kindness to let you know," and then took her departure.

Mrs. Bradley was ready to descend, when she heard a violent scream.   Instantly rushing down stairs, she found her sister lying on the floor in a deathly swoon.   She was a woman of rare, cool judgment, and knowing it was only a faint, she placed her on the sofa, loosened her clothing, and then ran for a bottle of ammonia she had in her valise. Presently her sister partially recovered, and looking wildly around, she cried: "Oh, Kate! was it some horrible dream? No, there is the paper," and turning her face to the wall, she gave way to an uncontrollable fit of weeping.

On picking up the paper the elder sister instantly defined the cause of her terrible grief. Headed in large display type, she found the following announcement:

"Fearful Tragedy! A Cold-Blooded Murder! Another Victim of the Rum Traffic!!"

"About two o'clock this morning, a drunken row occured in Sweeney's saloon, corner of Fifth and Cedar streets, resulting in the murder of a young man named Frank Steele. It appears that Steele and Harry Wardsworth, who, a few years ago, was a promising lawyer in Cedarville, but at present is noted only as a drunkard and a gambler, had been drinking together, when they got into a quarrel as to who should pay for the drinks. Wardsworth called Steele a mean scoundrel; whereupon the fight commenced. During the struggle, Wardsworth dealt his antagonist a powerful blow which felled him to the earth, striking on the curbstone, from the effects of which he died at five o'clock this morning. Wardsworth is in jail, awaiting the result of the coroner's inquest. There is no doubt but he will be committed to await the action of the grand jury."

On reading the above, Mrs. Bradley could only exclaim, in the fullness of her heart, "My poor, dear sister, I fear this blow will kill her. Thank God, that I am here to afford her, at least, some little comfort."

After a while the stricken wife grew calmer, and turning to her sister, said: "Kate, I want you to look after little Harry. I am going to the cell to see my husband." Mrs. Bradley questioned the wisdom of such a course, but finding her determined, consented on condition that she should lie perfectly quiet until breakfast was prepared and then should take a cup of tea and some toast. This done, the devoted wife set out on her journey to that dark abode of sin and suffering which contained the dearest of all her earthly treasures.

On giving her name she was readily admitted, and following her guide she passed along the dark corridors, through the darkness and vileness, past low, coarse vulgarities, and foulmouthed obscenity, where were incarcerated alike and together, the low, hardened criminal, and the victim for the first time fallen beneath the power of the tempter, only to learn more evil, and to go out a still greater adept at crime. Clinging closer to the arm of her guide, she passed on until, at last, she stood at the door of her husband's cell. The policeman unlocked the door, and merely saying, "Here is a lady wishes to see you," permitted her to enter. A

look of mortal agony passed over the husband's
face as he recognized his wife, and, for a moment, she questioned if she were not mistaken.
His face was so pale and haggard that it seemed impossible that the man before her was her
husband. But when in accents of indescribable
anguish he asked, "Oh Belle, my wife, why did
you come to this terrible place?" her doubts
were all removed, and for answer she fell
weeping on her husband's breast. Only for a
moment did she give way, then with a strong
effiort at self control she replied: "Why did I
come here, first because I felt it my duty to
come, and second because I could not help it.
Harry, you are my husband, and I have sworn
to stand by you, for better or worse, till death
parts us, and God giving me strength I shall do
it." As she said this, a look of unutterable
sympathy came into her face, and parting the
still jet black locks, she imprinted a pure kiss
on his once manly brow.

Long they talked, he telling her all he knew
about the sad affair. In her heart she knew her
husband was no murderer, nor yet a gambler.
He was the victim of a traffic sanctioned and
upheld by law. A foul, moral crime; and though
the sad consequences might be visited on his
head, it would be but another victim added
to the many who were being continually sacri-
ficed on the unhallowed altar of the rum traffic.

Strange to say, from her sad visit, and even

from the overwhelming calamity itself, she
seemed to gain strength. She still clung to the
belief in the power of God, and faith clung to
Him as her refuge and hope. Perhaps, she
thought, even this last crowning sorrow may be
made the means of salvation. Thus strengthened, she turned away from the abode of misery,
leaving behind her a pure and holy radiance,
as if some angel from the far away glory had
passed by.

As was predicted, the coroner's inquest made
short work of the case, and the jury had no hesitation in sending out their verdict that "Frank
Steele came to his death at the hands of Harry
Wardsworth, and recommending that the said
Harry Wardsworth be held without bail to await
the action of the grand jury." That body, of
whom Slocum chanced to be foreman, after, as
that worthy gentleman expressed it, "going
very carefully over all the facts in the case,"
rendered a true bill and Wardsworth was committed, to take his trial at the next term of
court.

Wardsworth was so far subdued that he
looked upon all the legal proceedings with
indifference, never once making any effort to
take any advantage on points of law. He
seemed, in fact, like one in a dream. To all
who questioned him on the subject, he made
but one reply. "I have not the slightest knowledge of the transaction. I know that I had no

enmity in my heart toward Steele—that I wished him no wrong, and I am not, therefore, morally, a murderer, whatever the law may make of me. I claim no palliation, but am ready to let the law take its course. Only for my wife and child, the sooner it is over and I am out of the way, the better. Though, God help me, I fear I am a curse instead of a blessing to them."

Still there were many friends who had known him in his prosperity, and who resolved not to turn against him even though he was deep down in the valley of adversity. Prominent among these was Dr. Thornton, of whom mention has been previously made, and Thos. Sherwood; the latter, a wholesale merchant, and a man of extensive wealth. He was, moreover, a noble specimen of the christian gentleman. His wife, too, clung to him all the more closely, frequently visiting him in his cell, and always meeting him with a cheerful smile, even though her own heart was breaking.

There was yet nearly three months before the court would sit, and his friends hoped for good to result from waiting. It would give him an opportunity for reflection. Possibly by that time, he might get control of his appetite and gain strength to overcome his foe. Of his final acquittal they had no doubt. Thus the days went by, sadly and slowly, each one bringing its own burden of sorrow.

CHAPTER VIII.

THE CUP FULL.

Solomon Slocum, Esquire, had finished his somewhat late dinner, had smoked his cigar, and was ready to make his usual afternoon visit to his distillery and dark cellar, when the door bell rang and a lady was announced. Being admitted into the library, the Squire returned her salutation somewhat awkwardly, and requesting her to be seated, prepared himself to listen to what she had to say.

"I understand, Mr. Slocum, you hold a mortgage on the residence now occupied by the family of Harry Wardsworth." At the mention of Wardsworth's name, Slocum started, and a look of uneasiness became very apparent. Recovering himself, however, he put on a bold front and replied: "Yes, I have a mortgage on it, and have been repeatedly advised to foreclose, but out of sympathy for the family I have let it run. I would have very much preferred to have Mr. Wardsworth redeem it, and save it to his family, and have told him so, but, perhaps as you are aware, the poor fellow has fallen into very unfortunate habits, and I fear will never be any better."

" I think I know something of his habits, Mr. Slocum, and also the unfortunate influences by which he has been surrounded;" and she fixed her gaze steadily upon him; "but it is about the mortgage, not about his habits, that I came to talk with you."

"Yes, yes, madam! Well, as I was saying, my sympathy for the family has kept me from foreclosing, but I think I shall do so now."

"I am the sister of Mrs. Wardsworth, and I came at her request to inquire how her husband came to give you the mortgage and on my own behalf, to get all the information concerning it possible."

For a moment Slocum winced. This was touching a subject that he did not wish ventilated. So, after clearing his throat once or twice, he replied:

"I am hardly prepared to give you the full information now; I can only say, in a general way, that the most of it was for cash advanced, though a small part was for book account. Did you wish to take up the mortgage?"

Mrs. Bradley—for it was no other than she —saw at once that it was useless to question him, though satisfied that the whole business was a fraud. Doubtless, however, he had been sharp enough to make himself secure in his villainy, and as she did not wish to parley where no good could possibly result, merely replied:

"It was not for that purpose I called; but to confer with you about surrendering the place to you. My sister informs me that you proposed to her, to pay them five hundred dollars, and take the property. Is that correct?"

"That is correct, madam. I did make such an offer."

"I am glad to learn that much, Mr. Slocum," replied Mrs. Bradley, with a slightly tremulous voice. "As you know my sister is in deep trouble; and five hundred dollars would be of almost untold value to her now. We proposed to get one or two friends to go with you, if you will be kind enough, to the prison, and pay the money to Mrs. Wardsworth, and her husband, I am sure, will sign any papers that may be necessary? I am here on a visit from New York State, and desirous of helping her to move and get settled in some comfortable little cottage before I return." This also had the effect of making Slocum feel uncomfortable. He had scarcely expected the matter would come up in this shape, though it would have to come out and he might as well meet it now as any time. With another throat clearing he answered:

"Really, my dear madam, I am surprised at your request. I wonder that Mr. Wardsworth did not inform his wife before of the state of the matter. The truth is, the five hundred dollars has already been paid to him, and I hold his receipt for the money, and also an agreement signed and witnessed, to vacate the premises whenever I shall give him ten days notice."

Mrs. Bradley was almost overcome with disappointment and chagrin; but rallying herself in a moment she answered:

"My sister was not aware of that fact, Mr. Slocum, or I would not have troubled you. While I am here, however, will you please let me look at the receipt and agreement?"

"I am very sorry to disappoint you in that, Mrs. Bradley, but they, with the rest of my papers, are in the hands of my attorney, Hon. Hezekiah Simkins.

Mrs. Bradley saw that nothing could be gained by extending the interview, so apologizing for the trouble she had given him, she withdrew.

But the disappointment was terrible to bear. How could she go back and convey the sad intelligence to that already heart-broken woman, that the last dollar of their beautiful home had been swallowed in the awful ruin? That she and her boy were helpless beggars and her husband in a criminal's cell? She could not do it.

Oh! rum traffic, thou cruel monster, thou destroyer of innocence, thou weapon of the tyrant and the right hand of him who would trample to the earth the helpless and defenseless. Thou slayer of the lowly, and the scourge in high places, as there is a God who rules on high, thy doom is written, and the day of thy destruction comes.

Such were the thoughts of Mrs. Bradley as she wended her desolate way back to her more desolate sister. No, she could never bear to that dear, suffering one, the last drop that would fill her cup of bitterness. This she would do. She had one hundred and fifty dollars of her own with her. This amount she would give, as though it had been given by Slocum, and explain that the balance had already been paid to her husband. Even this appeared like mocking at her suffering, but it was the best she could do. Her husband, she well knew, would approve the act, and she would have time to write home for sufficient for her expenses before she would need it for returning.

Leaving Mrs. Bradley, to carry out her noble resolution and explain matters in her own way, we ask the reader to accompany us to another scene. Almost at the very hour in which Mrs. Bradley was making her visit to Slocum, the following conversation was going on in the counting-room of Mr. Sherwood:

"I say, Sam," remarked one clerk to another, "Did you hear that old Slocum had got his fingers on that beautiful property of Harry Wardsworth?"

"No. Is it true, though? How did you hear it?"

"Only a few nights ago I was at the Opera. Jim Slocum and young Brooks, both of them somewhat the worse for liquor, sat right behind me. I was not an eavesdropper, but they talked so loud I could not help but hear what they said."

"What did Slocum say of it?"

"Oh! he was boasting of his old man's smartness, as he called it. He said he was too smart for Wardsworth, that he had got him in a tight place and had got a mortgage on his residence, and Wardsworth had agreed to surrender the property for five hundred dollars. 'But you bet,' added Jim, 'the old man is smart enough to cheat him out of that. If he can't beat him out of the five hundred, and get it that way, he is going to foreclose, and turn them out into the street. You bet the old man knows what is what. The mortgage is only seven thousand, and didn't cost the old man that, and the property is worth ten, at least. Oh, let old Slocum, as they call him, alone. He is smart enough for any of them.'"

Mr. Sherwood overheard the conversation and he was indeed startled. This was the first intimation he had that Wardsworth's property was so seriously involved. If this were true,

what would become of the wife and boy?
Somehow, as a christian man, he felt a responsibility he could not throw off.   Why should
poor Wardsworth and his family be left entirely
at the mercy of the avaricious Slocum? Suppose
they were driven into the street, would his
conscience be clear, remembering that he was
Wardsworth's friend? These thoughts passed
rapidly through his mind, and quickly his resolution was taken.   True, he had but little to
hope for from Slocum, in whom avarice was
the ruling passion; but he could at least try.

It was true, as young Slocum said, the
property was worth ten thousand dollars, for
the family.   It was at least worth the effort.
Even if nothing else could be done, he would
place the amount of the mortgage in the hands
of an attorney and let him act for Wardsworth
in taking up the mortgage.   On the latter's
honor he felt he could rely to secure him till
such time as they could sell the property.

And so it was that scarcely had Mrs. Bradley
retired from her interview with Slocum, than
the bell again rang, and Thomas Sherwood was
ushered into the presence of the burly distiller.

"I say, Slocum," remarked Sherwood, "I called
over to make some inquiries relative to Wardsworth's residence. I am told you have a mortgage on it."

"Yes, I have a mortgage on it."

"What is the amount of the mortgage?"

"Seven thousand dollars when given. The interest makes it more than that now."

"What interest does it draw?"

To use a homely phrase, Slocum began to smell a rat. He in no way liked these close questions. Evidently Sherwood's visit boded him no good, and the less he allowed himself to be pumped, the better. So pausing a moment, as if in thought, he answered:

"I can't say what the interest is now. The papers are in the hands of my attorney, Simkins."

"Strange," said Sherwood, "that you don't remember how much interest the mortgage bears. What will you take for the mortgage, cash?"

"Do you want the property for yourself, Mr. Sherwood?

"No, I do not. I want to save a home for poor Wardsworth's family. Come now, Slocum, let it be known that you have done a noble act. You shall have all the cash for it. I will give you the face of the mortgage, cash. What do you say?"

"I consider the property worth ten thousand dollars, Mr. Sherwood. Don't you think so yourself?"

"I presume it is. That is the reason I wish to save it for them. That will give them some three thousand dollars clear, or enough to purchase them a comfortable little home."

"You seem to take a great deal of interest in Wardsworth's wife, Mr. Sherwood; more than he does himself, I reckon," and the man gave a low brutal laugh. "If you want to buy the property for her, you can have it for ten thousand."

At any other time and place Sherwood would have resented the gross insult, and have dealt out to the villainous wretch, summary vengeance. But now, he was on an errand of mercy, and had a benevolent purpose to serve, and he passed it by with the remark, "I can do better than that, Slocum, and I will, too. You had better get your papers all ready, for in less than two hours from now the cash will be in the hands of Harry Wardsworth to pay the mortgage."

"It will, will it? Perhaps I may be allowed to inform you that Harry Wardsworth don't own the property. I have a deed for it, and a written agreement signed by him to vacate it, at any time, on receiving ten days' notice. What do you say to that, Mr. Sherwood? You will have to buy Wardsworth's wife a house somewhere else, I reckon," and again he gave that low, insulting laugh.

"What have I to say to that, Solomon Slocum? I say you are either an infernal liar or an infernal scoundrel, or both. I say, moreover, that you dare not go to the prison and look your victim in the face. You dare not go to the home of which you have robbed him, and

look into the face of his suffering wife, whom
you have made the subject of your brutal jest;
a person who in purity and true virtue is as far
above your whisky bloated self, as God is purer
than Satan. I say further, that you dare not
go down with me to Simkin's office and show
me all the papers you hold against Wardsworth.
I say still further, you dare not tell me, just,
truthfully, how you became possessed of that
mortgage. And further yet, that you got it by
fraud, that you got poor Wardsworth down to
Simkin's office, that you got him drunk, and
then and there put into operation a plan that
would put to shame the Devil himself, by which
you robbed him of his home and sent him out
a beggar. That is what I have to say, Mr.
Solomon Slocum, Esquire."

"It is a *lie*." shouted Slocum, "*an infernal lie,*
and I will cane any man that dares to utter it,"
and springing to his feet, he propelled his un-
wieldy form over to where Sherwood was
standing.

"Softly, Slocum! softly, my dear sir! Remember you are built more for drinking liquor than
for fighting, and like it a great deal better.
You had better calm yourself. I have yet one
or two things to say before I go, and I will say
them now."

' "You won't, I say. I won't listen to any more of
your infernal lies. You've insulted me in my own
house, and I bid you get out of it. Do you hear me?"

"Certainly, Squire Slocum, I hear you, but you forget that you gave me the first insult. I intend to do your bidding presently, and leave your house; but not until I have finished my answer to the question you asked me some time ago. You asked me what I had to say to it. I have told you in part, please do not interrupt me till I have finished. I said you have robbed poor Wardsworth of his home. You feel comparatively safe, because you know it would not be worth while to expose his failings and disgrace his family, besides wasting in law what little there is left that your rapacity has not stolen from him—hence you will probably pass into possession. But let me tell you, Slocum, there is yet a God in Heaven, and sooner or later swift and awful retribution will overtake you. Why, you poor coward, you are trembling like an aspen, even now, in the presence of a man like yourself. What will you do when God rises up to judge you for your robbery of the poor, and to visit upon you the awful punishment for your crimes? You asked me what I had to say. I have told you. Go you now and take poor Harry Wardsworth's home. Turn his wife and child into the street, but remember and prepare for the just retribution that is sure to overtake you;" and Mr. Sherwood walked out, leaving Slocum the most sadly disconcerted man in the city of Cedarville. In fact he scarcely knew whether he was dead or alive. The first thing he did was to go to his cupboard and take down a bottle and pour out a glass of brandy, which he drank. Not of his own manufacture. He knew too much about what he made to drink that. This done, his courage revived, and looking to see that all the doors were shut, he muttered: "Confound it, here is a pretty kettle of fish. How did that fellow, Sherwood, ever find out about that mortgage? I am just in time in getting the property. True, as he says, they will not be apt to do anything, as the matter stands, and if they do, I have Simkins and Bradshaw fast enough. They will both swear they saw me pay the money over to Wardsworth. That will fix that. Hah! Sherwood, old Slocum is a little too sharp for you there."

"True, Wardsworth's wife has not signed the deed, and, in the absence of her signature, there will be a cloud on the title. I will fix that all right however. Wait till her drunken husband is either hung, or sent to prison, and I will soon fetch her to time. Nothing like starvation for bringing proud people to terms. Let her have her choice between signing the deed, and the alms house and a few hundred dollars will secure her signature, and fix that all right. As I don't want to sell the property, I can afford to wait."

"But that retribution business is what upset me. Heavens! he talked like a preacher. I haven't stopped shaking yet. I guess I will take a little more brandy, that will set me right again," and suiting the action to the word, he took another stiff drink. "Now I feel better. I must go and see Simkins and have him issue the notice for them to vacate the premiess at once." In doing which, we will leave him to his own reflections.

CHAPTER IX.

THE BLACKNESS OF DARKNESS.

Mrs. Bradley carried out her noble resolution and her sister never suspected the sacrifice she had made. While bitterly lamenting the loss of her beautiful home, a feeling of devout gratitude went up to God that even that small amount was saved to her. The house had so many sorrowful associations connected with it, that she could leave it with far more resignation than under different circumstances. In fact, the loss of their home and all other troubles seemed to be swallowed up in the one great sorrow arising from the condition of her husband. Were he the noble, manly man he was when they were wed, a home in a hovel would be a palace compared with their present condition.

Still she did not lose all hope, but through all the accumulating sorrows still clung to the belief that at *some time* all would come right again.

Oh hope, thou most precious boon to mortals given. Without thee, how dark, how gloomy would be our life's journey. Thou dost bid the heart take courage even when every prospect fails. Thou dost cheer the weary pilgrim, bind up the heart that is broken, paint the darkest cloud with a silver lining, and mingle sweetness even with the most bitter cup. Thy radiant finger points to brighter scenes beyond, and thy cheering voice makes the drooping spirit rally. Without thy bright presence earth would be desolate. Despair would fold her gloomy mantle over all, and voices of anguish unutterable would chant the funeral notes of the world's sorrowful dead.

Mrs. Wardsworth had finished her morning work and had sat down for a few moments rest, when the door bell rang, and a strange gentleman was admitted—or at least we will call him that, in the absence of any known classification to give him. He was short and stout, with a very red, bloated face, and a most villainous expression of countenance. Without heeding the polite invitation to be seated, he stood for some minutes fumbling in his pockets, and then produced a note, and handing it to Mrs. Wardsworth, remarked: "Here's a letter for yer, and I was told to wait and see yer read it, so I could swear yer got the notice to vacate, supposing they had to put the law on yer." Mrs. Wardsworth took the missive and read as follows:

Notice to Vacate—To Mrs. Henry Wardsworth:
—You are no doubt aware that I hold a deed
of the property now occupied by you, and an
agreement signed by your husband to vacate
the same at any time required, on receiving ten
days' notice. You will please, therefore, vacate
the residence at once. Signed,

SOLOMON SLOCUM.

By his att'y, HEZEKIAH SIMKINS.
Dated at Cedarville,——. 18—.

Mrs. Wardsworth glanced over the document
and then handed it to her sister, merely remarking to the bearer, "You can say to Mr.
Slocum that the property will be given up to
him without any delay on our part."

"I guess yer better," replied that worthy official, "'cause old Slocum has no mercy on a
feller when once he gets him in his paws."
And with this comforting remark he left the
two sisters to arrange their plans as best they
could.

"Well," said Mrs. Bradley, "I suppose, sister, we
must look the matter squarely in the face. The
first thing to do is to find a suitable house. I
am stronger than you, and will go out to look
for one and let you attend to little Harry, and
she immediately commenced her preparation.
At that moment the door bell again rang, and
Mr. Sherwood was admitted. He had often
been there before and his visits had always

brought sunshine. A brighter atmosphere seemed to pervade the room as soon as he entered. Without any false modesty he immediately announced his errand.

"I learned a day or two ago, Mrs. Wardsworth, that your property here had passed into the possession of Slocum, and that you are required to vacate it. Is that correct?"

"It is, Mr. Sherwood: We have just received the notice to do so this morning," and she passed him the note. Mr. Sherwood read it over and with a smile, remarked, "I see, Slocum has but one style of doing business with all. But I consider it somewhat fortunate, Mrs. Wardsworth, one of my tenants has just vacated a house that I think will suit you. It is a very comfortable house of seven rooms, and on a good street. If one of you can go with me I shall take pleasure in showing it to you."

Thus, even in the darkness, there appeard a ray of light. Mrs. Bradley accompanied Mr. Sherwood and found the house more than they could desire. "As for the rent," said Mr. Sherwood, "I will arrange that with Mr. Wardsworth after he gets through with his trouble. I consider it very fortunate that it is vacant just at this particular time."

Mr. Sherwood did not explain *how* it became vacant. He did not say that he had paid the tenant fifty dollars to have him move out of it; but such was the fact, nevertheless. Ah, no, he did not say that; but He, who knoweth all things, knew it. He who watcheth the sparrows' fall, had seen it all, and over against the name of Thomas Sherwood had written, "Inasmuch as ye have done it unto one of the least of these, ye have done it unto me."

Both Mrs. Wardsworth and her sister were deeply affected by this exhibition of true generosity; and when that night they knelt together in their evening prayer, side by side, with their petition for grace for the erring husband, went up the earnest supplication that blessings might descend upon the head of their benefactor.

The next thing was to move, and they decided to do that the day after to-morrow. They had sufficient furniture left to furnish the cottage comfortably, and together they could make it a very cosy, comfortable home. The next day they received a call from Mrs. Sherwood. She came, she said, to go over to the cottage and see if they desired any change, and putting on their wraps, and taking little Harry in his carriage, they set out. Mrs. Wardsworth appeared more cheerful than for months. She even joined in the laugh that arose, and entered with something of her old cheerfulness into her sister's plans for furnishing the cottage.

Somehow, Mrs. Sherwood succeeded in learning all the sister's plans; some slight changes were suggested which it was concluded would take one or two days to complete, so it was decided to postpone the moving for one day longer. Before leaving, the visitor secured a promise that the sisters would spend the day after to-morrow with her. The carriage would call for them early and they must come prepared to spend the entire day.

According to promise, Mrs. Sherwood called in person for her friends, and so far as it was possible under the circumstances, Mrs. Wardsworth enjoyed her visit. When night came they were prevailed on to remain till morning.

"I am very sorry, Mrs. Wardsworth," remarked Mr. Sherwood, next morning at breakfast, "but we did not succeed yesterday in getting our work quite finished at the cottage. If we can prevail upon you to remain with my wife to-day, I am sure it will be ready for you to-morrow. Perhaps Mrs. Bradley could ride over with me in the carriage, and give a little instruction on one or two points." To this arrangement Mrs. Wardsworth consented, although the time dragged heavily. She was now more than ever anxious to leave a place so full of painful memories and retire to the quietness of her cottage home.

After breakfast Mr. Sherwood and Mrs. Bradley drove over to the cottage, promising to be back to dinner. It was late when they returned, and consequently, that evening tea was served a little later than usual. As Mrs. Wardsworth declined to remain longer, the carriage was ordered and the two sisters were driven home. Somewhat to Mrs. Wardsworth's surprise, the carriage was driven in the direction of the cottage, Mrs. Bradley explaining that she left a parcel there she wished to get. On arriving it was proposed that they go in and see how the changes suited. On reaching the house, Mrs. Wardsworth uttered an exclamation of astonishment. Everything was done. The carpets were down, stoves up, beds arranged, all the furniture in its place, and everything in perfect order for housekeeping, with no necessity for going to the old place again.

At this exhibition of thoughtful kindness Mrs. Wardsworth was overcome, and throwing her arms around her sister, wept tears of gratitude.

"Oh! it is so thoughtful and kind of you, sister. What would I do in this hour of my soul's dark trial were it not for you?"

"Please, sister, do not give me the credit for it. It was Mrs. Sherwood's plan, and I only entered into it. She is a noble christian woman, I think." ·

"She is truly. How true it is, sister, that the bitterest cup contains some drops of sweetness, and the darkest cloud may have a silvery lining Oh, if Harry were only here, and with this dark cloud lifted from him, this cottage would be a paradise. But oh, how my poor, weak faith does sometimes waver and my weary feet almost refuse to walk the path so thickly crowded with thorns. Kate, do you think it possible that so dark a night can ever know a morning?"

For answer, Mrs. Bradley drew her sister's head upon her breast, and gently stroking the throbbing temples, said, as if in meditation:

"It was a dark tempestuous night. Hour after hour the storm had raged on Geneseret's lake. The weary disciples had put forth every effort in vain. The wind blew more fiercely, the billows rolled higher, and the frail craft, tossed about more wildly. Shipwreck and death stared them in the face. In this hour of their peril they came to their Savior. 'Master, carest thou not that we perish?' It is enough. The Savior but looked out upon the tempest and breathed the gentle command, 'Peace, be still,' and lo! there was a great calm. Belle, that same Savior is saying to you, 'Come unto me all ye that labor and are heavy laden, and I will give you rest.' I know how dark your pathway has been, and I do not know how much deeper may be the darkness through which you will yet have to pass; but I do know He has said, 'I will never leave thee nor forsake thee.' Your faith has been sorely tried, and may be tried yet more severely, but as you have so faithfully believed and so nobly trusted, do not let your hope forsake you now."

Thus did the loving sister and wise counsel-

lor instruct and comfort, till at last, she had
the pleasure of seeing the wavering faith
again reassert itself, and looking up smiling
through her tears, her sister replied: .

"Bless you, dear Kate, for those words of
encouragement and hope.   I do feel that come
what will, God is too wise to err, and too good
to be unkind.   I will trust him, even though he
slay me."

"And now, dear Belle, I must begin to talk of
leaving you.   I have been with you several
weeks, and I feel as though duty calls me back
to my loved ones in the east.   It is hard for
me to leave you in your sorrow, and I still think
it would be better for you to go with me, but
at the same time, my heart approves your strong
determination to stand by your husband to the
last.   I shall probably leave you in a few days,
but remember Belle, whatever betides, your
place in our home is open for you, as that in
our hearts is already filled."

"Oh I know, Kate, how dear I am to you,
and how cheerfully you would receive me; but
for the present, I have but one thought, and
that is for poor Harry.   I shall lay no plans for
the future, but hope and pray, if it be God's
will, that he will restore me my husband.   If
that cannot be done, that he will give me grace
to bear whatever his hand may send me.   And
now, as it is late, let us retire.   To-morrow I
must go again and see Harry.

The days swiftly sped and the time arrived for Mrs. Bradley to return. Indeed, she would have started a day or two before, but little Harry had been unwell, and she did not wish to leave. Now, however, he was better, and the next day was set for her departure. But that night there came another messenger. He came, notwithstanding the doors were barred and the windows fastened. He stole in noiselessly, and they dreamed not of his coming until he had gained admittance and his cold breath was felt upon the cheek, and his icy fingers grasped the strings of life.

About midnight Mrs. Bradley was awakened by her sister. "Come into my room, Kate, and look at Harry. He is making such a strange noise, and I do not know what is the matter with him."

Mrs. Bradley hastily threw on a wrapper and went into her sister's room. She found the little fellow apparently sleeping, but his breathing was labored, and with each inspiration there was a sort of crowing sound.

"What do you think is the matter with him, Kate?"

Mrs. Bradley did not answer for a moment, but presently she said:

"Belle, do you make a fire as quickly as you can, and get some water on to heat. I will dress and go for Dr. Thornton. I fear the child has the croup. We have no time for lamentations or hesitation. This must be met promptly, and hastening to her room she was very soon ready for her visit to summon the doctor. Fortunately, that gentleman had just returned from a visit, and had not yet retired. Answering the bell himself, he was surprised to meet Mrs. Bradley. She quickly delivered her message, and stated her fears relative to the case, and asking him to come at once, hurried back without waiting for him.

Dr. Thornton awakened his wife, and asking her to arouse James, the servant, and send him up in case he might be needed, hastened at once to the sick chamber.

There was no mistaking those symptoms. They pointed too unmistakably to that terrible disease—croup.

By this time the servant arrived, and hastily scribbling a note he directed the servant to carry it to Dr. Nichols. It read as follows:

"*Dear Doctor:*—Come at once to 255 Cedar street, and help me in a severe case of croup. *We must save* the patient."

In a very short time Dr. Nichols arrived, and then the battle commenced in earnest. Dr. Thornton's treatment was approved, and together the two physicians bent all their energies to arrest the dread disease. Oh, what a mortal struggle! On the one side sympathy, reputation, science and knowledge, and on the other fell disease. All night long the struggle continued, the helpless mother looking on the terrible scene in an agony of hope and fear. Never did science put forth more noble efforts, and never did she have a more stubborn and deadly foe to contend with.

When the cold gray morning stole into the room and lighted up the haggard faces of the lone watchers, it found the struggle ended. The vanquished representatives of science who had so nobly fought with Death, stood looking with solemn, speechless sorrow on the result of the conflict. Their eyes rested only on the cold dead form of what, but yesterday, was the fondest hope and joy of his suffering mother, litttle Harry Wardsworth. The form was there, the same sweet smile rested on his countenance, but the childish laugh was silent, and the arms that so often loved to twine the mother's neck, lay peacefully folded across the breast, for little Harry Wardsworth was dead. Beside the dead form the mother sat, looking down upon it with cold tearless eyes. "Oh God," she cried, "surely thou hast brought me into the blackness of darkness. Oh, Kate! what great sin have I committed that I should suffer thus terribly? Can it be that even God, in whom I have trusted, has risen up against me?" and she gave way to her unutterable anguish.

Gradually she became calmer and suffered herself to be removed from the room, and Mrs. Thornton, who had been summoned by her husband, and Mrs. Bradley, set about preparing the body for its last resting place.

The suffering mother sought the quiet and privacy of her own room. There, in the early morning, another messenger found her. Found her kneeling at the vacant crib, with hands up-lifted and streaming eyes upturned to Heaven. It was the messenger of Peace. He had caught the ascending prayer and bore it up to the Throne of the Eternal. It fell upon the ear of Him who never yet hath said to the seed of Jacob, "Seek ye my face in vain." The Comforter came down, and taking his place beside the kneeling, suffering pleader, set the seal of Divine peace upon her heart. Above the storm was heard the Divine promise, "I will never leave thee nor forsake thee." Faith again mounted above the thick darkness and rested upon God. When she came down from that "secret place of the most high," how changed! The look of despair had given place to one of calm resignation and trust.

How peacefully slept her dead! How "safe in the arms of Jesus!" She felt that her loving Father had done wisely, although she could not trace the wonders of his hand. Stooping down and pressing a kiss upon the dear dead face, she exclaimed. "The Lord gave and the Lord hath taken away." "Oh, help me, Father, to bow in meekness to thy chastening rod." Faith had triumphed where science failed, and "underneath her were the everlasting arms."

The next day was the burial, and kind friends came in and took sole charge of the arrangements. Sherwood and Thornton selected a beautiful lot in the cemetery, and after arranging for the digging of the grave, went to break the tidings as gently as possible to the incarcerated father. They made an early call, first on the Judge, and then in company with that gentleman, on the sheriff.

"Davis," said the Judge, to the sheriff, I have a mind to grant the request of these gentlemen, if you will allow me to assume the responsibility, and allow Mr. Wardsworth to go and attend the funeral of his child. I know the risk we run in doing so, but it is for humanity's sake. I believe we can rely on Wardsworth's honor. The result was that they all repaired to Wardsworth's cell, and how it all happened no one ever knew, but when they came out the prisoner accompanied them.*

While Sherwood took Wardsworth with him for a complete change of clothing, Thornton went to the cottage to convey the news of his coming; and so it happened that two hours before that appointed for the funeral service, the stricken wife and mother was permitted to lean, weeping, on the breast of her husband, as

*An occurrence similar to that above described was known to the author in 1860.

together they looked down upon the peaceful face of their dead.

At two p. m. the friends assembled for the last rites. They were those who had known Harry Wardsworth in the days of his prosperity, and who had been his fast friends all through his downward career. Those who had labored for his recovery, and who even yet hoped for the best. Not one of his companions in dissipation was there. They had drunk of his wine, had pledged him in the cup, in the better days of his prosperity, had partaken of his generosity, but now, in his humiliation, not one was there to speak a word of comfort. Even thus cruel is rum to its victims.

The funeral service began, and the voice of the aged minister grew tremulous with emotion as he read the beautifully solemn words of the Episcopal burial service. "Man that is born of woman is of few days and full of trouble. He cometh forth as a flower and is cut down." He continued reading to the end, and the service was concluded. Still no one moved. A spell seemed to be upon all. The silence became oppressive. The pastor laid aside his ritual and bowed his head in extempore prayer. His prayer became more earnest and his voice more tremulous as he prayed for the tempted and erring father. Oh! how he plead that Omnipotence might come to his deliverance ; and as he prayed, his listeners caught the inspiration of his faith, and from many a lip was heard the low, fervent "God grant it." He prayed for the wife and now childless mother. That her faith might not fail her in this hour of her extremity. Again the listening spirit caught up the petition, and it was treasured in the book of God's remembrance.

The funeral service was closed and the dear little form left to its peaceful sleep in Rosebloom cemetery. An hour or two at home and then Wardsworth must return to his cell. He had pledged his honor that he would do so, and that pledge should be kept inviolate, whatever the consequence might be. But who shall tell the result of that hour, amid the solemn influences of his home, still filled with the radiant presence of a living faith, even amid the solemnities of death. What sad retrospects! What lookings forward? What sins repented of, what resolutions made? What backward longings over joys departed, what aspirations toward a purer and a better life? Who shall tell what thoughts of prayer went up, or what assurances of comfort and strength came down upon his soul? Ah! none may enter into the sacred sanctuary of that, save him who knoweth the hearts of all, and who permits not one earnest desire after good to fall unheeded in his ear. Suffice it to say, when the evening shadows gathered and the stars came out, one by one, the sad adieus were spoken, and Harry

Wardsworth took again his prison garments and went back to his solitude and his cell.

Mrs. Bradley now, more than ever, thought to prevail on her sister to accompany her home and remain, at least, till time for Wardsworth's trial, which would not come off yet for several weeks. To this, however, she would not consent. To all Kate's arguments she would answer, "please sister, do not urge me. God has kindly taken care of little Harry, and now I have nothing to do but to give my life wholly to my husband. Oh, Kate, my dear sister, you can't tell how, with what loving, longing sympathy my heart yearns toward him now. If the sacrifice of my life could be but his ransom, I am ready to lay it on the altar. More than ever he needs my presence near him, and more than ever am I now in a position to minister to his wants and to influence him for good. Please, dear Kate, don't think me ungrateful," and she wound her arms tenderly around her sister's neck and raised her tearful eyes to her face— "but I can't leave my husband."

Finding it useless to urge her further, the elder sister prepared for her departure. The hour of separation came, the last farewell spoken, the last impassioned kiss given, and Mrs. Bradley was borne swiftly away, leaving the heartbroken wife and childless mother to take up anew the burden of her sorrow and carry it alone.

CHAPTER X.

THE TRIAL.

Let not the reader imagine that during all the events recorded in the last chapter, Harry Wardsworth, or his future welfare, was treated with indifference. His wife had continued to make him regular visits, and strove by every art in her power to lift him up to a higher plane of thought. Sherwood and Dr. Thonton, with others, also interested themselves and made every needful preparation for his trial, as well as to arouse the better energies of his nature, and thus prepare him for the new struggle in which he would have to engage after his release.

As for Wardsworth himself, he seemed almost to have lost all interest in life. He would sit for hours apparently in deep meditation, unless aroused, and then would answer so vaguely, and in that listless sort of a way, which showed his mind to be occupied with something else. His friends saw very clearly, that if left to himself to prepare for trial, he would be almost completely at the mercy of his enemies, and set themselves resolutely to work, resolved that he should have simple, impartial justice, and they asked nothing more.

One morning the Hon. Hezekiah Simkins was surprised by a visit from Sherwood.

"Simkins," said Sherwood, "I have called to see if you will allow yourself to be retained for the defense of Wardsworth in the approaching trial."

"Really, Mr. Sherwood, I am sorry to disappoint you, but I do not think I can take the case for the prisoner."

"And why not, will you allow me to ask?

"Well," and Simkins looked uneasily around, for several reasons. "In the first place, there is no disguising the fact, that Wardsworth is a poor, drunken, reprobate, and whoever has anything to do with him must expect to lose his hold on respectable society."

"Not necessarily, Simkins. I have stood by Wardsworth all the way through, and intend to stand by him to the end. I have not yet lost my respectability, and do not think there is the least danger of doing so. So far from that, I have always regarded it as pre-eminently respectable to stoop down to human wretchedness and help to raise the fallen. As to your fee, you need have no fear about that. I will see it paid."

"Oh, I don't mind the fee, so far as that is concerned, but to tell the truth, I have promised to assist the state's attorney in the prosecution."

"Ah! then you are retained against him. So, putting your theory and your practice together, they amount to this: You believe Wardsworth to be a poor drunken outcast, of whom the sooner the world is rid of the better, and acting on that belief, you have arranged to do your share toward accomplishing that end. Now my belief is just the reverse of yours, and therefore my action directly opposite. I believe Wardsworth yet possesses the elements of a true and noble manhood. I believe also, that there is sufficient hope in his case to warrant the most gigantic efforts to save him; and acting on that belief, I am bound to make such an effort. I am glad, however, to know you will be there, for we shall want you for an important witness for the defense."

"I, an important witness? And pray, what do you expect to prove by me? I know nothing about the case."

"Not so fast, Simkins. I think you do know a good deal about the case. And now, to answer your question, we expect to prove by you where Wardsworth first became intoxicated on the night of the killing. We expect to prove by you how Slocum came to get possession of Wardsworth's home. We propose to prove by you just where he was up to the hour when we first find him at Sweeney's saloon. In short, Simkins, we propose to prove by you, to the satisfaction of the public, if not that of the law, at whose door lies not only the killing of Frank Steele, but the ruin of Wardsworth as well. Since you will not allow yourself to be retained as counsel, we shall take advantage of your presence and you as a witness. Be sure and be present, Simkins, for we shall need you;" and taking his hat, Sherwood departed.

"I fancy that has settled the question so far as Simkins is concerned," said Sherwood to himself, as he walked away. "If my suspicions are correct, the state's attorney will have to look elsewhere for assistance than to Hon. Hezekiah Simkins. That shot told. If I thought there was the slightest prospect of his swearing to the truth, I would summons him, but he is such a rascal to begin with, and is so much under the power of Slocum, that I will not run the risk of making him perjure himself. If I can frighten him sufficiently to make him keep out of the way, that is sufficient."

Simkins was taken all aback. "This is a pretty medley," said he to himself. "A nice mess truly. On the one hand there is that five hundred dollars old Slocum promised me if I could convict Wardsworth, so as to get him out of the way, but on the other, I run the risk of convicting both myself and Slocum. I'm blessed if I haven't a mind to give the whole thing away. Wonder if Sherwood would not give a bigger fee to have me defend Wardsworth than old Slocum gives to convict him. The old scoundrel! I don't wonder he wants to get poor Wardsworth out of sight. Hah! I have it. I'll go to Slocum and tell him all that Sherwood has said. That he is going to put me on the stand and prove the whole transaction relative to the getting of Wardsworth's property. If I don't frighten him out of another five hundred then my name is not Hezekiah Simkins;" and seizing his hat he started for Slocum's office.

'I say, Slocum, what the mischief do you think is to pay now?"

"Why, what? Nothing bad, I hope;" and Slocum started up and turned pale.

"Only this, that the whole business of getting Wardsworth's property is out, and is all to be laid before the court at his trial."

"It can't be possible. Why, how could it? Who told you?"

"Sherwood, the wholesale merchant. He has just left my office. He says he knows all about it. I strongly suspect that that rascal, Bradshaw, has squealed. At all events he says he is going to put me on the stand and prove the whole transaction."

"But you won't swear to it, will you?" said Slocum, almost imploringly. The wily lawyer saw his advantage, and hastened to follow it up.

"Look here, Slocum," he said, "suppose Bradshaw has gone back on us, and he goes before the court and swears that you got that mortgage, and that last five hundred dollars on the night of the murder, by—well, as you did get them,—and suppose it should come out that I have not only aided you, but been guilty of perjury, will it help you any?"

"No, I suppose not. But what can we do?"

"Sherwood has been to me, also, and offered me a very large fee to defend the prisoner. He said he knew if I defended Wardsworth, he would be cleared; and then they should enter an action against you for fraud."

"How much did he offer you? Did you not tell him you were retained by the prosecution?"

"I certainly did, and he said that is just what he wanted, for he should put me on the stand. The fact is, Slocum, there is only one of two things can be done. I must either take the case for the prisoner, or you must make it worth my while to keep out of the way. Fortunately, I have not yet received a summons, and probably will not for awhile, as they expect me to be there."

The result of the above conversation was, that a few days before the expected trial, the state's attorney received the following note from Simkins:

CEDARVILLE, ——— —, 18—.

Dear Sir:—I very much regret that important business calls me to a distant part of the State, and that, in consequence, I shall be unable to assist you in the approaching trial of The People against Henry Wardsworth.

Very truly yours,

Hon. Hezekiah Simkins.

The writer of the above letter, with one thousand dollars of Slocum's money safely stowed away in his pocket, was conveniently absent from the trial.

A few days after the events narrated above, a number of Wardsworth's friends were together in Sherwood's counting-room. They were there by appointment to make definite arrangements for his defense.

"I say, Sherwood," asked Dr. Thornton, "what was the result of your visit to Simkins."

"It was so far satisfactory, that we may rely upon it, if Simkins is associated with the state's attorney in the case, our suspicions are not well founded. On the other hand, if they are correct, and I verily believe they are, Simkins and Slocum will both be afraid to face the fear of the consequences, and will be absent; and whoever argues the case can, in their absence, make a powerful argument in addressing the jury. I believe we have thrown a bomb-shell in the enemy's camp. At all events we have done a wise thing, and in any event a safe one. And now, gentlemen, whom shall we employ to defend the prisoner? I have a note here from one of my travelling salesmen, written from L——, some two hundred miles south, which I will read to you.

L——, ———, 18—.

THOMAS SHERWOOD, ESQ.

Dear Sir:—I have made the acquaintance of a lawyer here who volunteers to undertake the defense of Harry Wardsworth. I have taken pains to inquire into his standing, and find that he ranks very high in his profession. Moreover, he also has known the sad consequences of rum drinking, but he has been rescued, and is now a most earnest temperance worker. He only asks that his name be kept secret, in connection with the defense, especially from Wardsworth. The fee is of no consequence. I think he is just the man for you. Truly yours,

W. J. HARVEY.

The result of the above letter was, that the next train bore Sherwood to L——, the consequence of whose visit will be seen at the trial.

At last the expected day arrived. So great was the excitement and interest in the case, that long before the hour for opening the court, the room was filled to its utmost capacity, and hundreds were unable to gain admittance. Public opinion was somewhat divided as to the merits of the case. Some, and they were of the class who generally followed the lead of such men as Slocum, regarded it as nothing less than cold-blooded murder, and insisted that nothing short of imprisonment for life would satisfy the claims of outraged law. Others, taking a more lenient view, argued that the death of Steele was not the result of the blow, but the fall; and as Wardsworth had no intention to murder, the most that could be made out of it would be manslaughter. Still a third class, and these the most intelligent of all, looked upon both Steele and Wardsworth as but the victims, the former of legalized murder, perpetrated by the liquor traffic under the protection of law.

At the appointed hour the Judge took his seat, the court was opened, and the first case on the docket was found to be "The State against Henry Wardsworth, who stands charged with the murder of Frank Steele."

"Sheriff, bring up the prisoner;" and Wardsworth was placed in the criminal's box.

"Is the prisoner represented by legal counsel?" asked the Judge. At that moment there was a movement in the audience, and a gentleman came forward, and taking his place at the table, said with a smile: "May it please the court, I believe I am to represent the prisoner."

Instantly every voice was hushed and all eyes were bent upon the strange lawyer. He was an entire stranger, never having been seen in Cedarville before. As he stood there in the consciousness of intellectual power, he was not a man easily forgotten. He stood at least six feet high, and well proportioned. His complexion was dark and his face was covered with a full, black beard. His eyes were jet black, set far back in his head, and his hair, which was also black, was thrown back from his brow, revealing a massive forehead.

Although he did not look at the prisoner, his presence affected Wardsworth strangely. He leaned forward and bent on him a long, earnest gaze, like one fascinated. Presently, he seemed to recognize him, for falling back on his seat he buried his face in his hands and remained for a long time as if lost in deep thought.

The greater part of the first day was spent in selecting a jury. The counsel for the defense challenged but few. So long as they bore the evidences of intelligence and respectability, he seemed content to let them pass. The state's attorney, on the contrary, was evidently determined to reject every juror who he thought was not prejudiced against the prisoner. For this reason he questioned every juror called, and put every question allowed by law. Thus the first day was so nearly consumed that the Judge decided to adjourn the court and commence the examination of witnesses in the morning.

The court room was filled the next morning even earlier than the morning before. At the usual hour the prisoner was again placed in the dock and the trial commenced. We have not space to give the report in full, and therefore content ourselves with a short summary, which is all that is necessary to our purpose.

The principal witness was Sweeney, the saloon keeper. He testified that Wardsworth came to his saloon about one o'clock A. M. on the night in question, and was intoxicated when he came. Several others were there, among whom was young Steele. They drank several times, Wardsworth paying for the liquor. About two o'clock Steele called for liquor, and he and Wardsworth, with one or two others, drank. Steele refused to pay for it, and, after disputing for a while, Wardsworth paid for it, but remarked, "Steele is a mean scoundrel, and I will never drikn with him again." At that Steele challenged Wardsworth to fight; which the latter refused to do, and started for the street, saying he was going home. By this time he was quite drunk. Steele followed him and threatened to strike him, saying, "I'll cut your heart out," or words to that effect, and made a rush at Wardsworth, who, as he came up, dealt him a blow in the face, knocking him down. As he fell he struck the back of his head on the corner of the curb stone, and lay there apparently insensible. When picked up he was speechless. Witness also testified to finding an open knife on the ground where Steele lay, which was recognized as belonging to deceased.

Dr. Edward Garrison testified that he was

called to see deceased about three a. m. Found him in a state of profound coma, in which he continued till his death, about five a. m. Found blood oozing from a wound in the back of the head, about three inches long. The occipital bone was crushed in and rested on the base of the brain, which was ruptured, and was also oozing out through the wound. Evidently death was caused by the wound in the occiput. Found, also, a lump, as from a blow, on the left temple.

To prisoner's counsel: A fall with the back of the head striking on the curb stone would make such a wound as that found upon deceased. The blow on the temple was evidently not sufficient to cause death.

The prosecution called, also, a number of witnesses to prove that Wardsworth was of a quarrelsome disposition, and that he really began the quarrel with Steele; but in this they failed. At this point the prosecution rested their case, and the counsel for the prisoner addressed the court.

"May it please the court, there are two courses open for me in this case, and I am in some doubt which is the wiser one to pursue. To pursue the one would no doubt be best for my client; to pursue the other, I have strong hope would be better for our cause. I am persuaded were I to move that the prosecution has failed to make out a case, and that there is nothing to go to the jury, you would rule in my favor,

no doubt agreeing with me, that the prisoner
acted solely in self-defense. Indeed, I must express my astonishment that, with the facts as
presented before this court, there could be
found a grand jury in the country who could
be induced to find a bill. I am convinced that
the prisoner is the victim of a foul conspiracy,
which has seized upon this unfortunate circum-
stance to rob him of his freedom or his life.
It is barely possible that we may be able to
unearth some of this conspiracy before we get
through, and I will, with your permission, allow
the case to proceed, and accept the verdict of
the jury."

The Judge nodded approval, and the counsel
called as his first witness, Hon. Hezekiah Simkins.
"Hezekiah Simkins! Hezekiah Simkins!" shouted
the crier. "He fails to respond," answered that
official.

"This is somewhat strange," said the counsel.
"We did not think it necessary to summons the
Honorable gentleman, because we were informed
that he was certainly to be here. In fact, that he
was associated with the state's attorney against
the prisoner. May I ask the attorney if that is
correct?"

"You certainly may ask it," he replied, "but
I am not certain that I am required to
answer."

"Oh! as you choose about it. I will not press
the question, as I think I can satisfy the jury

of the correctness of my statement through other means. For the present I will call Solomon Slocum. "Solomon Slocum! Solomon Slocum!" shouted the crier.

"He, too, appears to be *non est*," remarked the Judge.

"May it please the court," replied the counsel, "I confess this is passing strange. I am informed that both of those gentlemen have been the principal movers in pressing this case against the prisoner. That Mr. Slocum was the foreman of the grand jury who found the bill against him, and Simkins was retained to assist in the prosecution."

"May I ask the counsel," remarked the Judge, "what he expects to prove by those witnesses? If it is relevant, we can adjourn the case until they can be summoned."

"I presume," answered the counsel smiling, "the relevancy of the testimony would be a question for your decision. In answer to your question: We expected to prove just where the prisoner was and who were with him on the night of the killing, previous to his arrival at Sweeney's saloon. We proposed to show what influences were used to get him in that condition, and the motives for so doing. In short, we proposed to prove to the satisfaction of the jury that the visit to Sweeney's, the drinking there, and the death of poor Steele, were but the consequences of other crimes committed by other parties, and that the direct responsibility of this death passes over beyond the prisoner, and rests on those other parties, just as the fall was the result of the blow. But as there is no one on trial for this crime but the prisoner—though it is my firm conviction there should be,—and as those witnesses are not absolutely necessary to the perfect vindication of the prisoner, with your permission I will waive the motion for an adjournment and allow the case to go to the jury, making my argument solely on the testimony as presented by the prosecution."

To this also the Judge nodded assent, the audience, by their movements, signified their approval, and the jury settled themselves to hear the war of words between the two legal champions.

The state's attorney opened the argument. He began by stating to the jury how painful to him was the duty he felt called upon to discharge. A duty so painful that nothing short of the deepest sense of obligation could induce him to undertake it. The task was all the more painful, because the criminal was himself a brother of the law. He referred to what the prisoner once was. He began at the time of Harry Wardsworth's popularity as a lawyer and traced the history of his fall. Unfortunately he had given himself up to vicious habits. Lower and lower he had fallen in the scale of human degredation, until he had become an outcast and a reproach to the society in which he had once moved; a companion only of the lowest and vilest. At last he had reached the climax of his shame and brutality, when without provocation, he had with one blow felled to the earth an inoffensive young man and thereby caused his death. "Gentlemen of the jury," said he, "the dignity of violated law demands that the murderer be punished. Such a man is not safe to run at large. The safety, the well-being of society demands that such monsters in human shape be held strictly accountable for their fiendish acts. Let the law take its course; let society be protected, even if it requires the law to rid the earth of one who has so far thrown away his manhood as to afford no hope of his ever again rising above the level of the beast. I leave the case with you, satisfied that the prisoner will receive justice at the hands of outraged law and an intelligent jury of his countrymen." The attorney closed his argument, having occupied one hour and forty minutes.

The state's attorney was one of the most successful pleaders in the State; and his address made a strong impression, alike on the jury and the audience. A close observer could have seen that Wardsworth felt his remarks very keenly indeed.

The counsel for the defense arose amidst the deepest stillness of the vast audience. He cast a hasty glance over the assembly, and it seemed to thrill them like an electric shock. Bowing to the court, and then looking steadily into the faces of the jury, he began his address. His voice, though low, was so modulated that it was heard distinctly in every part of the large room.

"May it please the court and gentlemen of the jury. In the course of a somewhat extended practice, it has never before been my lot to be placed in a precisely similar situation to that which I occupy to-day. Before us stands a man who is on trial for the terrible crime of murder. I stand up in your presence to argue the case for the prisoner, without calling a single witness for the defense. I trust that you will regard the fact that I do this, as sufficient evidence of two things. First of my unbounded confidence in the justice of our cause; and second, as the highest possible assurance I can give you, of my perfect confidence in the righteousness of American law. This is the reason why I have declined to act on the very kind suggestion of the court, to move for an adjournment of the case, but the rather, to refer it directly to the wisdom and justice of an intelligent American jury.

"In arguing this case, gentlemen, let us see wherein the counsel for the people and that for the defense agree. We agree in the fact that a murder has been committed. Of that there can be no dispute. It needed not the evidence of

Sweeney, nor the ghastly story of the surgeon, to prove it. Its proof is seen in that silent mound of earth that now rises in Rosebloom cemetery. In the silence that alone answers when is called the name of Francis Steele. In the desolation of that home where weeps the broken-hearted mother. Ah! yes, we admit the fact that another murder has been committed, and another is added to the long catalogue of crimes whose very heinousness might well cause the angels to blush for the fallen sons of men. But, gentlemen of the jury, I deny that the guilt of that crime, the blood of the murdered Frank Steele, rests upon the prisoner at the bar. It is but another added to the long list of murders committed by the same monster, whose bloody hand has already robbed Harry Wardsworth of his home, shorn his manhood of its strength, broken the heart of his wife and made her a childless mother, and has now placed him in a criminal's dock to answer to a charge of murder which that monster's own hand committed. I repeat, gentlemen, I deny, and that on the very evidence offered by the prosecution, that the prisoner is guilty of the crime laid to his charge. The indictment charges the prisoner with having wilfully and maliciously, and with malice aforethought, taken the life of Frank Steele. On this point let us review the evidence. And please bear in mind gentlemen, that all our evidence is adverse; we

have none save what has been presented by the
prosecution.   According to their testimony,
the prisoner came to Sweeney's about one
o'clock, A. M., and he was then intoxicated.
Gentlemen, I want you to notice this fact. The
prosecution made no effort to enlighten you as
to where he came from, or by what influences
he had been surrounded.   Had the gentlemen,
whose names I called been present, I believe
we could have satisfied you on that point, but,
luckily for themselves they are conveniently
absent.   Could we but have the privilege of
putting them in the box, we believe we could
bring to light a conspiracy against Harry
Wardsworth, that would put to blush the
Arch-fiend himself.

The prisoner comes to Sweeney's saloon at
one o'clock, A. M. and finds it open and the proprietor doing business.   Why is that business
establishment open at that hour of the night?
Were there any other business establishments
open at that hour?   Were there any stores
open, with the proprietors behind their counter?
Were there any of our mechanics' shops, our
blacksmiths, our coopers, our shoe or wagon-
makers in their shops at that hour?   No!
gentlemen.   Persons engaged in a respectable
calling had long since closed their places of
business and were wrapped in the slumbers of
honest men. It was the hour and the business of
darkness.   The prisoner comes to the saloon and

finds others there drinking. He was already intoxicated, but this particular business establishment was open and the proprietor behind his bar ready to wait upon his customers. His wares were temptingly arranged upon his shelves and hanging upon the wall, was the regular legal authority by which he did his business. The demon that was within Wardsworth's breast, the appetite that had been created by authority of law, craved for more drink. As I said, hanging there on the wall of Sweeney's saloon, was the printed document, bearing the seal of authority, which bore testimony to the fact that on the payment of one thousand dollars, he was duly and legally authorized to sell that which the prisoner craved. The demand for the commodity was therefore a legal demand; a demand created by the authority of law. The sale which Sweeney made to supply that demand was a legal sale, a sale made by the authority of law. The purchase which the prisoner made was a legal purchase. The result of that legal purchase on the one hand, and the legal sale on the other to supply a legally created demand, was that the prisoner became so much intoxicated—legally intoxicated, mind you, intoxicated according to law—that he became unconcious of his acts, and was therefore not responsible. Up to this point then, every step that we have traced. as presented by the prosecution has been legal, and Harry Wardsworth is in a state

or irresponsibility, made so by the authority of
law.

"We will now proceed another step.   In this
condition Steele asked him to drink yet once
again. Again there was a legal sale on the one
hand and a legal purchase on the other.   And
right here gentlemen, we have the evidence that
stamps as unjust and untrue the statement of
the counsel for the prosecution, that the prisoner had thrown away his manhood.   For this
liquor, purchased by Steele, not by Wardsworth,
the former refused to pay. Now, what did the
prisoner do? Did he, too, refuse, as he might
have done? No.   On the contrary, he paid for
it himself, merely remarking that Steele was a
mean scoundrel, and he would have nothing
more to do with him, a remark that was certainly justified by the facts.   Does this justify
the counsel's statement that the prisoner had
thrown away his manhood? No, gentlemen.
Had the counsel been half as anxious to deal
out simple and impartial justice, as to convict
the prisoner, he himself would have seen the
evidence that contradicts his statement.   Even
in his besotted condition, his God-given manhood
rose superior to the degradation and asserted
its dignity. We admit that a moral crime,
sanctioned by law, had robbed his manhood of
its strength, but the manhood itself was not
lost then, and is not lost now, and it depends
upon you, gentlemen, whether or not the pris-

oner, by a life of earnest, noble effort, shall have the privilege of contradicting the slander of the counsel, that Harry Wardsworth has thrown away his manhood.

"The next step is, the prisoner is challenged by the deceased to fight. Did the prisoner accept the challenge? Did he manifest the least evidence of a quarrelsome disposition? No. Not one tittle of evidence has been produced by the prosecution to prove that Harry Wardsworth ever began a quarrel in his life. On the contrary, he started immediately for his home. Would to God, gentlemen, that he had not left it on that fatal night. Would that the smiles and songs of his wife, the childish prattle of his now dead boy, had possessed sufficient power to break the chain, that a cruel, designing foe had thrown around him.

"The deceased followed him into the street, and there, drawing a knife, threatened his life. Then it was that the fatal blow was struck. Another evidence that the prisoner had not thrown away his manhood. The same inherent manhood that prompted him to pay for the liquor that he had not ordered, prevented him from running away, like a coward from the man, who in his drunken frenzy would rob him of his life. In pure self-defense, without any malice toward, or any desire to do bodily harm to the deceased, he struck the blow which felled him to the earth, where, striking on the corner of the curb-stone he received the wound which caused his death.

"Here then, gentlemen of the jury, is the ground on which we base our plea of not guilty. It was an act of self-defense, warranted alike by every principle of manhood, and the laws of our country. The prisoner did just what you or I would have done were we perfectly sober. The only difference there is, he did it as an act of instinct, himself being unconscious and not responsible, we would have done it as an act of reason and have held ourselves ready to answer for the responsibility. Hence, gentlemen, you cannot find a particle of authority in the law, nor justification in your own consciences for the conviction of the prisoner of the crime of murder.

"Here, may it please the court and gentlemen of the jury, we might, with the most perfect confidence, rest our case, certain of the acquittal of the prisoner; but we have not yet accomplished all that we have desired. We have admitted that a murder has been committed, but we believe we have satisfied you, that for that murder the prisoner at the bar is not guilty.

"The question then arises, who is guilty? In a legal sense we are not bound to answer that question, but I trust the court will give us a little latitude. On whose skirts shall we look for the blood of poor, murdered Frank Steele?

Nay, more than this. We not only admit the murder of Steele, but we say there have been two murders. In that same cemetery are two new made graves. The one is that of the deceased, Steele; the other is a shorter grave, and holds the dead form of the prisoner's boy. It is that of his only child. The dear, darling boy; the one tie that bound the parents yet to life and hope. We charge the murder of these two victims upon the legalized liquor traffic of the country. We charge it with robbing the prisoner of his home. We charge it with robbing his manhood of its strength. We charge it with the living torture and slow, cruel murder of his wife. We arraign it before a righteous God, and charge it with being the archfiend of murder. We point to seventy thousand dishonored graves, all made in the last year, and charge it with first the degradation, and then the murder of every occupant of those graves. We point to seventy thousand more victims and say, before the end of the year it will have murdered all these. We point to seventy thousand homes now wearing the habiliments of a great sorrow, and charge it with having sound its slimy folds within the sacred precincts of those homes, and laid its murderous hand upon some of its loved inmates. We arraign the legalized liquor traffic before the bar of consistency and demand its condemnation by every principle of moral right and common intelligence. We bring as our witnesses, first, the statutes themselves. What say they? They testify that the liquor traffic is a legal, lawful business. That it is recognized as such by every statute for its regulation and protection. Here is a man authorized by law to sell a certain article. When the customer buys it, he makes a legal purchase; as much so as though it were, instead of the slow, deadly poison it is, a sack of flour, or a barrel of beef. Moreover, he buys that liquor to drink. The law expects him to drink it. The man who sells it is authorized to sell it for that very purpose. The man drinks it and it makes him a maniac. It robs him of his reason and destroys his responsibility as a citizen. In this condition, a condition made such by law, he commits a crime; a crime of which he is no more conscious than the maniac in an asylum, and then the law takes him and hangs him, or sends him to prison for life, which is equally as bad, if not worse.

Gentlemen of the jury, do I put this too strongly? Let the case of poor Cook be the answer. You all knew that man. He lived in your midst; he was your neighbor; known and respected until his manhood was lost through the influence of the legalized liquor traffic. First, it robbed him of his eyesight, and he became so nearly blind that he could not work. You all knew his disposition. When sober, he was a lamb, but when drunk, he was a demon.

When sober, there could be no more loving husband, no kinder father. When himself, he was
as innocent and harmless as a child. The
liquor traffic was his sworn and bitter enemy.
It had already robbed him of everything but life itself. Now, what ought the
law to have said and done in that case? It
should have thrown around that poor man the
shield of its protection. It should have risen up
in the dignity of its might and said, I will protect this man from the further attacks of his
most deadly foe. But did it do that? No, gentlemen. Instead of this, it joined hands with
the man's enemy. He came one day to the city,
and what did he find? He found over twenty
business houses, in every one of which there
hung a printed certificate bearing the official
seal, stating that the keeper thereof was duly
authorized by law to sell him that very thing
that had already proved his ruin. Authorized
by law, there was a bargain and sale. He made
a legal purchase and the business man made a
legal sale, as he was legally authorized to do.
True, the supporters of this foulest blot upon
the fair fame of our beautiful and beloved
country, stand ready to question this statement,
and to answer—"Does not the law provide that
the saloon keeper shall not sell to an habitual
drunkard?" Admitted—but does it not continue to issue its legal authority to sell this
liquid death, just as it has done for a hundred

years, well knowing that their only customers are those who are more or less drunkards? That if they do not sell to that class, every last man of them must either starve, or be driven to some decent employment? You remember when Mrs. McDonal, a lady of refinement and culture, went to those same twenty saloon keepers, and on her knees * implored them not to sell liquor to her husband, who was a drunkard, nineteen out of the twenty, pointed to their license as their authority and answered, that they paid for the privilege, and that was the way they made their living. The statement, therefore, that the law, in this respect, protects the drunkard, is the basest of falsehoods.

Cook drank the liquor and it robbed him of his reason. He became a maniac; as much so as any member of an insane asylum in the land, and no more responsible for his acts than they. He went home. His wife came to meet him at the gate. Like most other insane people, he imagined his best friend to be his worst enemy.

Seizing a sled stake he struck his wife a blow which felled her to the earth and laid her dead at his feet. The wife of his youth lay dead, and he knew nothing of it till he came to himself the next day in the jail. Here, then, was one murder committed by the traffic which

---

*This lady, and the incident referred to, were alike known to the author.

the law sanctioned and protected. Then
what did the law do? Was it satisfied, now
that one victim was legally murdered? No. On
the contrary, side by side with the law that authorized this legal purchase and sale, which resulted in the murder of Mrs. Cook, appeared
another law, and again we find the statutes
joining hands against the poor victim of the
rum traffic. Now comes this second law, and
grasping the poor maniac by the throat, it said:
"You are a murderer and you must die." It robes
itself in its judicial vestments, and taking its
seat on the bench of justice, goes through the
form of trial. It pronounces the victim guilty,
with the sentence that on a certain day he shall
be taken to the place of execution and hung
by the neck until he is dead, and may God
have mercy on his soul! Oh! solemn mockery!
Not satisfied with one legalized murder, the law
must have two. The day of execution arrives.
The gallows is erected. The victim is placed upon
it, and the last words he uttered on earth were his
dying protest that he had not the slightest
knowledge or remembrance of what he had
done from the time he left the city till he found
himself in jail the next day. Still that makes
no difference in the estimation of the law. The
word is given, the bolt is withdrawn, the drop
falls and Cook's body rolls one way and his head
another. The dignity of the law is satisfied,
but instead of one, two more murders are

registered in Heaven's court against the legalized liquor traffic.*

"Here, then, is a case, and hundreds more might be cited, illustrating the inconsistency, yea, the heinousness of the liquor traffic, and the laws regulating the same. To that already long list of murders have now been added those of Frank Steele and poor little innocent Harry Wardsworth. For ask Dr. Thornton, and he will tell you that the death of that boy was the result of a cold, caused by moving into the cottage so soon after repairing and plastering. Who robbed them of the beautiful home they had, and made moving necessary? I need not answer the question, for the facts are too painfully evident before you. And are not two deaths enough? Must there be added still a third? The answer to these questions will be given by the verdict you will this day render.

"Gentlemen of the jury, I have done. In closing. permit me to remind you that you occupy those seats as the representatives, the agents of the law. The law in this case can act only through you. It pronounces its utterances through your lips. If it condemns the prisoner and confines him to a felon's cell or a dishonored grave, making him another victim, it is only because you say it shall so be ordered. If it says to

*The above is given just as it occurred, without changing the name.

this victim, 'Thus far shall thine enemy come, but no farther,' if it utters the language of mercy and says, 'Go and henceforth show how noble is the manhood I have saved,' if it turns to that heart broken wife and says, 'Here, I give you back the husband I have rescued,' it will be because mercy, and wisdom, and justice dwelt in the heart of the twelve men who sat as its representatives. Can you look into the face of the prisoner at the bar, on whose hands and in whose heart there is found no stain of blood, and say, 'You are a murderer?' Can you look into the face of that pale, heart-broken, childless mother and say, 'Your husband is a murderer?' Can you stand beside the grave of that darling boy, and looking down upon that silent mound, say, 'Here lies the child of a murderer?' Can you hold in your hands that most sacred of all sacred trusts, committed to you as citizens, the ballot of an American voter, knowing that there rests upon you a common responsibility, as those who stand behind our laws and give them force and power, and yet as the representatives of those laws, say Harry Wardsworth is a murderer? No, gentlemen, I have no such fear. I have endeavored to do my duty, not only to my client, but to my country as well, and now leave the fate of the prisoner in the hands of an enlightened jury of his countrymen."

The counsel sat down amidst breathless silence, having held the audience, as if spell-bound, for over two hours. The state's attorney waived his right to sum up, prefering to let the case go to the jury.

The Judge charged the jury, dwelling at length on the aggressive attitude of the deceased, and somewhat strongly justifying the plea of self-defense. After reviewing the evidence he closed as follows:

"There can be no question, gentlemen, as to the truth of all that has been advanced by the prisoner's counsel. Indeed the half has not yet been, and never will be told. I have never yet sat through a term of court that I have not felt myself humiliated, as I have been called to administer the penalty of the law for the very crimes which are the legitimate fruits of itself.* There are on our statute books to-day, no laws so inconsistent, so cruel, as the laws that regulate and uphold the liquor traffic. There is no source of crime more bountiful. There is no such swift road to poverty. It is filling our poor houses with paupers, our prisons with criminals, our asylums with insane. It is filling our cemeteries with the graves of its murdered dead. What the terrible end will be, unless the people recognize the evil and meet it, where it can only be successfully met, at the ballot-box, I dare not anticipate.

"I shall not detain you further, gentlemen,

---

*The precise words of the learned Judge Wilson in 1868.

but allow you to retire and consider your verdict."

The jury retired, and though it was 10 o'clock P. M., not a person left the court room. It was evident to all that they would be but a short time making up their verdict. The Judge remained on the bench and the counsel retained their seats at the table. The prisoner sat upright, apparently unmoved, but a close observer could have detected evidences of deep, but suppressed emotion. His wife sat just where she had done all through the trial, with Mrs. Sherwood on one side and Mrs. Thornton on the other. During the whole course of the trial she had not wept, save when the counsel had referred to the death of her boy. She had already drained the bitter cup to the very dregs, and would no longer shrink, whatever might betide.

Fifteen, twenty minutes—a half hour passed, and yet the jury tarried. Scarcely a sound was heard, and the silence became painfully oppressive. Presently the door was opened, and the word was passed, "Make way for the jury;" and the twelve representatives of the law filed in and took their seats on the jurors' chairs.

"Gentlemen of the jury," said the clerk, "have you agreed upon your verdict?"

"We have," answered the foreman.

"What say you, gentlemen of the jury? Is the prisoner at the bar guilty or not guilty?"

Clear and distinct was heard the answer in every part of the room, "Not Guilty."

Instantly, in spite of every effort to prevent it, there was a scene of wild confusion. The clapping of hands, the waving of handkerchiefs, and even hearty cheers were heard and seen all through the court room. It was some minutes before order could be restored. During the excitement the prisoner's counsel sat with his face buried in his hands. When order was restored, and he arose in his place at the table, it was noticed that his face was as pale as that of the dead.

"May it please the court," he said, in a voice tremulous with the deepest emotion, "I move for the release of the prisoner."

"The sheriff will release the prisoner," said the Judge; and Harry Wardsworth walked forth a free man.

Mrs. Wardsworth was the first to meet him as he stepped down from the dock. She did not faint or go into ecstacies; but, drawing his head down, she pressed on his cheek a kiss that told alike the devotion and joy of her heart. Presently, releasing himself from the embrace of his wife, Wardsworth hastened to where his counsel was standing watching the scene, and throwing his arms around him, he leaned his head on his shoulder and wept tears of penitence and gratitude. Thus did he meet his old friend and classmate, Harry Ferguson.

Friends now crowded around him, and for a time he was almost overwhelmed with the congratulations of those who had so long borne the burden of anxiety.

We will not dwell on the going home. How Sherwood and Thornton, with their wives, and Ferguson, made up a party that lasted till beyond the wee small hours. How the wife stole away to her little sanctuary, with a heart overflowing with gratitude, to lay her thank offering on the altar of her God. How the two lawyers sat and talked, reviewing their old acquaintance; Ferguson explaining how he came to hear of the case, and volunteer for the defense. It was a scene never forgotten in the lives of the two lawyers.

The early morning train was to bear Ferguson back to his home; and when he and Wardsworth reached the depot they found a number of the latter's friends awaiting them, among whom were Sherwood and Thornton. The former calling Ferguson aside asked for his bill, adding, "Don't hesitate to name your price, we have the money for you."

"Simply my expenses," replied the lawyer, the balance you can place to the credit of my vow, to strike the liquor traffic a blow whenever I have an opportunity."

The train at this moment drew in, the hands of friendship were again grasped, and Harry Ferguson was away, bearing with him the gratitude of happy hearts.

CHAPTER XI.

The trial of Wardsworth had one very beneficial effect. It aroused the temperance element in the community as it had never been aroused before. The public mind had received new light on the qeustion of the liquor traffic. The address of Ferguson and of the Judge, at the trial, had opened their eyes to the glaring inconsistencies of the laws regulating the sale of that which produced such dread results.

The individual responsibility of the voter never had been presented as the counsel presented it, and never had so deeply impressed them. The people not only comprehended the truth, but felt its power. The result was, men of all shades of belief, both political and religious, came together and resolved that all other questions should be considered secondary to the one great question of saving the people from its degrading and destroying influences. The various existing temperance organizations received fresh impetus and all worked together for one common purpose. The ladies met and organized themselves into a Women's Christian Temperance Union, which speedily became a power for

good.   The ministers of the various churches
arranged to preach a series of sermons against
the evil.   A column was secured in each of the
city papers, to be devoted exclusively to temperance agitation.   A course of lectures was pro-
vided for and the ablest speakers possible secured to deliver them.

The whisky men saw the storm gathering
and at once set themselves to avert it.   As
usual, the first thing they did was to call a convention.   Sweeping resolutions were passed, de-
nouncing the tyranny and fanaticism of the
temperance party.   They pledged, themselves,
their time and money to the task of defeating
the temperance work in every shape and form.
Religion did not trouble them, for generally,
they had none; but their political opinions were
by solemn resolution laid completely aside for
the time being, until this great temperance
fight was finished,   No political candidate for
any office, it was resolved, should have their
vote unless his sympathies were with their in-
terests and he would pledge himself to vote in
their favor.   Thus the fight went on, with each
succeeding week growing more and more determined.   Never was a there a more deadly
struggle, never did right and wrong, good and
evil, meet in more terrible strife.   Which shall
triumph?

Three months had now passed, and during
this time Wardsworth had remained perfectly

sober. His condition, however, gave the greatest apprehension. He seemed to have lost almost all his interest in life. The dormant energies of his mind seemed to defy every effort to arouse them. His ambition was gone, his spirit broken. For hours he would sit looking apparently at nothing, or wander aimlessly from room to room, when at home, and when absent therefrom appeared as if in constant fear. His health, too, had become very much impaired. The long season of confinement, the severe mental struggle through which he had passed, the terrible grief over the loss of his child, all combined had told heavily on his constitution and robbed him of his vitality. A sort of settled melancholy fastened itself upon him that caused his friends, sometimes, to fear the direst consequences.

Still, they never for a moment forsook him; but, on the contrary, the greater the cause for alarm, the more resolutely they labored. They sought business for him, but he performed his duties only in a mechanical sort of way, and often made mistakes, showing plainly that his heart was not in his work. Once when Sherwood, thinking to rally him, said pleasantly, "Wardsworth, what has become of your thoughts?" he rebuked him by answering, sadly, "They are with my hopes, in the grave of my dead boy."

The mental strain upon his wife was terrible

in the extreme. She lived continually in a state
of mingled hope and fear. Her cheeks grew
paler and her step more languid. Still, by
constant watchfulness, she was able always to
meet him with the same sweet smile, appearing
always cheerful, even though her heart was
filled with sadness. There was with her now
but one thought, and that was the complete reclaiming of her husband. For this she labored
and prayed with an earnestness that, it seemed,
must prevail. Her home was made just as
pleasant as it was possible to make it. She
studied her husband's every wish, anticipated
his every want, adapted herself to his various
moods, and in every way possible, strove to lead
him out of himself and into a more healthy
mental atmosphere.

One fact gave her hope. He evidently recognized himself as being safer in her presence
and influence. He clung to her like a timid
child. Whenever called out, he would go with
her to the gate, and be there to meet her when
she returned. Sherwood had fitted him up an
office, and he would invite his wife to walk to it
with him, and come to walk home with him.
She looked upon this as evidence that he realized his weakness and was determined to continue the struggle, and was so far encouraged.
But his pride, his nobility was gone. Ambition
seemed dead. Could she but see those reassert
themselves, could she but lift from him that

dark shadow. which like a funeral pall, hung over him, she would have strong hope; but as day after day, and week after week passed, and no change, hope began to die out in her heart and despair to take its place. The time was passing; most of the lectures, from which she had hoped so much, had been given. At first he had accompanied her to those meetings, but latterly had preferred to remain at home. She had attended whenever he had appeared perfectly willing for her to go. Especially had she made it a point to attend the meetings of the Women's Christian Society. Here her own over burdened heart had found relief in sympathy and prayer. Often, as she listened to the prayers of those earnest christian women, and knew that their prayers and their efforts went hand in hand, she felt her faith encouraged and resolved never to give up the struggle.

About this time Wardsworth received a letter from his friend and late counsel, Ferguson. It was as follows:

"L——, ——, — 18—.

"My Dear Wardsworth:—When last I saw you at Cedarville, you requested me to write you giving you some of my experience relative to my recovery from the vice and habit of intemperance. I am most thankful to comply with your request because of the old, tried friendship that existed between us in those happy

college days at old Yale, and because I most
earnestly desire that you, too, my dear friend,
may be able to rise up and reassume the proud
position, which by nature and education you
are so well calculated to fill.

"Do you remember, Wardsworth, those old
days when we used to sit in the corner room,
at our old boarding place, and build castles in
the air? When all the bright and happy future of our manhood, seemed to be beckoning
us on, like some beautiful pathway, radiant
with the flowers of spring. You remember
what high hopes we then had? How bright
the future active, useful life seemed to appear.
And yet when I think of how near I came to
being wrecked and all those bright hopes forever blasted, my heart goes up in devout gratitude to him who in his infinite mercy, listened
to my deep imploring cry for help, and stretched
out his mighty hand to save.

"I am convinced, Wardsworth, that happy
and full of hope as were those days, it was
there that we made our saddest mistake. It
was there that we laid the foundation of all
the deep, sore trouble which our later manhood
has brought us. You remember how we used
to laugh at what we were disposed to call the
weakness of those students who absolutely refused to taste wine. I used to think and I have
no doubt you did, that it indicated a sense of
weakness, a want of self control on their part.

That they were afraid to trust themselves, lest they should be overcome with wine. I used, from my heart, to pity them; but oh! all too sadly have I learned that they were right and I was wrong. While I devoutly thank God that I have been reclaimed, and now feel my feet firmly planted on the Rock of Ages, I cannot forget the dark way along which I have traveled, nor put away the scars I have received in my terrible struggle with the deadly foe I then received as a friend.

"You remember there was a band of total abstainers, as they called themselves, in the college. Well, so far as I can learn, there is not one of those but now occupies a position of proud eminence, while of all those who there learned to 'look upon the wine when it is red,' scarcely one but what has been stranded upon the dark rocks of intemperance. As I go over all the list of those once bright, promising students, and then remember all the blighted hopes, the crushed and bleeding hearts, and the dishonored graves, I think to myself: Oh! could my voice be heard by every student in the land, I would say, shun the wine cup; for however fair and sparkling it may appear, 'at the last it biteth like a serpent and stingeth like an adder.'

"You remember I wrote you from S., when I settled there, where I remained till four years ago, when I came to L. I soon worked up a good practice in S. I had hosts of friends who were willing to aid me in my efforts at advancement. No man of my age had a fairer prospect of success. Alas! but few have more sadly disappointed their friends.

"Unfortunately, my habit of drinking increased. The appetite grew stronger and more uncompromising in its demands. Still, like thousands of others, I refused to believe there was any danger. I laughed when my best friends warned me, and became indignant when they hinted the necessity of reforming. Strange as it may seem, with all the sad evidences to the contrary, I clung to the fatal delusion which has been the ruin of so many thousands, that a man may indulge the habit of drinking and yet hold his appetite under control.

"At last there came an awakening, and the terrible reality forced itself upon me, that I was a drunkard. Then began the struggle for my deliverance. But why need I recount to you, my friend, all the dark, bitter experience? Suffice it say, then only, did I learn how weak a man is, when once he has fallen beneath the power of rum. How weak I was; how powerful was the foe with which I contended. All my promises, all my resolutions were as nothing compared with the appetite that was consuming me. I saw my danger but had no power to avert it; I felt that the turning point had been reached; I felt that I must be rescued now, or pass beyond the limit of all earthly hope.

"In this condition I shut myself up in my room, resolved carefully and earnestly to review the past for the purpose of finding out where I had made the mistake, and of deciding on some plan for my deliverance. I soon found where I had made one fatal mistake, and resolved to rectify it at once. I had so far proceeded on the supposition that I could take one glass and then stop. This had been a sad, a terrible failure. If saved from a drunkard's fate, there was, I became convinced, but one course, and that was to abstain from even tasting or in any way associating with the fatal cup. This I resolved to do as the first step. Then and there I resolved, with the help of Heaven, never to taste another drop of liquor.

"Another thing commended itself, in fact appeared necessary; that was to connect myself with some good temperance organization and become an active worker in the cause. This, I reasoned, will put me in sympathy with the temperance element and I will have its encouragement and aid. It will also be a public declaration of my principles. So long as I am not pledged to temperance, my friends think themselves at liberty, and in some cases required to invite me to drink. But so soon as they learn that I have publicly pledged myself, no man who is my friend, and no honest man who is not my friend, will ask me to drink, and thus sacrifice my honor by violating a solemn obligation. And let me assure you, my dear friend, in this I have not been disappointed. I had no idea that the simple act of signing a pledge and becoming a member of a temperance society, could be of such real value to a man who does earnestly desire to break off from the drinking habit. It has saved me from a thousand temptations and done much toward planting my feet upon the solid rock, on which, I humbly trust, I am now standing.

"But this, I felt, was not enough. Though up to this hour I had never been, in the strict sense of the term, a religious man, yet I had been a believer in the bible, and in a vague sort of a way, in the power and benefit of prayer. But in that hour of my weakness, I felt its necessity more than ever before. Then it was that I remembered the lessons I learned at my mother's knee. They came with a vividness and force never possessed before. Floating over the vanished years, there seemed to come the sound of my mother's voice. I heard again the prayers she used to offer that God would bless and keep her boy. I resolved to test, in my own case, the power of prayer, which had ever been her refuge. Alone with God, I plead as only that man pleads who sees his terrible danger and feels that he himself is helpless. I tell you, Wardsworth, that was the holiest and most deeply solemn hour of my whole life. It was there I gained the victory over myself and my debasing appetite. I came forth from that solitary struggle with a strength and courage to meet my enemy, to which before I had been a stranger.

"As I look back upon it now, and am able to take a more philosophic view of my case, two facts are sufficient to solve the problem of my redemption. These are, first: I had reached the high ground of total abstinence, and a public profession of those principles before the world. I was thus in a position to meet my enemy at a point where I had all my powers and faculties at my command. I was no longer at so great a disadvantage. Heretofore I had to meet him after I had taken a glass or two, which only served to arouse the morbid appetite the more. Second: Hitherto I had relied solely on my own strength. I now came with a deep sense of my own weakness to look to that higher power, whose strength is made perfect in human weakness and is able to keep us from falling.

"The next evening there was to be a public temperance meeting. I went home a little earlier than usual and frankly told my wife what had been the burden of my thoughts, and that I had resolved to sign the pledge and once more be a free man. Oh, Wardsworth! could you have seen the sunshine which that assurance brought to the dear heart that had so long trusted and hoped. The joy of that one hour has amply compensated for all the sacrifices I have had to make in order to keep inviolate my obligation.

"There remains but little more for me to tell you. I fully believe I am a saved man ; and oh ! the gratitude of my heart at the thought of this is beyond expression. I believe I am safe because I am relying, not on my own strength, but on the strength that God gives to those who ask him. I am also actively working for the temperance reform. This keeps alive my interest, not only in others, but in myself and my own safety. If I may be the means of rescuing but one of my fallen brothers, it will be enough for a lifetime of toil.

"And now, my dear friend, I find I have written a much longer letter than I intended ; but I trust it may prove interesting to you, and perhaps be a source of some little encouragement in the terrible struggle you are now carrying on with the enemy. If aught in my experience can afford you instruction and hope, then let God be praised. I fain would aid you, if it were in my power. That you may have strength from on high, and yet come up from the deep darkness into the clearer, purer light, and to that grand and noble life of which I know you to be so capable, is my earnest prayer. Remember me most kindly to Mrs. Wardsworth and those other kind friends whose acquaintances I formed, and if at any time I can serve you, don't fail to command me.

"Your old friend and classmate,

"HARRY FERGUSON."

To say that Wardsworth read the above letter, would but poorly express the truth. He studied it point by point, and paragraph by paragraph, as he would some important legal document, on which hung great issues. Its effect upon him may be inferred from the following note, written in reply, a few days after:

"CEDARVILLE, ——, 18—.

"DEAR FERGUSON,—Your kind letter is to hand. I have read it and re-read it; and though my heart is too full to write much now, I cannot refrain from saying, it has done me more good than any other letter I ever received in my life. May God bless you, my more than friend.

"HARRY WARDSWORTH."

The same evening Mrs. Wardsworth had put on her wraps and got as far as the gate, intending to go to the office to meet her husband, when she saw him coming up the street. Something in his walk and appearance caused her to stop, and her heart to almost cease beating. There was something peculiar in his walk. Could it be the excitement of wine? or what was it that made his step so elastic? For a few moments

her heart was filled with sad foreboding. She
had been so often disappointed and cast down;
so often had her hopes been crushed, just when
she thought they were on the point of blossom-
ing into full fruition, that it was no wonder if,
on the slightest appearance of danger, her heart
gave a great cry of sorrow. A second look,
however, as he came nearer, caused her fear to
give place to a glad hope. It could not be the
effect of wine drinking. Somehow the look, the
step, and especially the smile, carried her away
back over the years of deep, dark sorrow, and
all unconscious of the sudden transition, set her
down in the midst of her departed joys. She
was conscious of but two things; her husband
was perfectly sober and everything about him
was changed for the better. And when he
came and stood by her side, and stooping down
imprinted on her forehead a husband's pure
kiss, just as he used to do in those long ago
happy days, she was gladder and happier than
she had been for long years. It was the first
bright beams of the morning, that heralded the
coming day.

"You were intending to go out this evening,
were you not," he remarked to his wife, as they
sat that evening at the tea-table.

"Yes, Harry, if you are perfectly willing.
You know this is the last meeting of our lecture
course"—and the voice grew slightly tremulous
—"and the woman's society has arranged for a

half-hour prayer meeting in the vestry, previous
to the lecture. But I will stay with you or go
out with you anywhere else, if you wish it," she
added pleasantly.

"I would rather you would go" he replied,
after a moment's thought. "Where did you say
the meeting is to be held?"

"In the Presbyterian church;" she answered,
and oh, such a longing filled her heart to have
him accompany her! But he had so often ex-
cused himself that she deemed it the wiser
course not to press the matter to-night.

Seven o'clock struck and putting on her wraps
and kissing her husband good bye, the brave, patient wife set out to meet her sisters in the good
work of encouraging the suffering of their own
sex, and so far as able, of rescuing the fallen of
either sex. The prayer meeting that evening
was one of the most interesting of the series. As
Mrs. Wardsworth looked over the little audience
and noticed how many wives were there whose
husbands had been rescued from the destroyer,
as she listened to the expressions of heart-felt
gratitude to God, for the great blessing that had
come to their homes, she felt that even if the
efforts in behalf of her own husband were not
successful, she could rejoice for what had been
done. She would not be selfish in her desire
or prayers. She would "rejoice with them that
do rejoice," and leave the whole of her own and
husband's future in God's hands. There came

over her a feeling of calm peace, and resignation and trust. An assurance that her Heavenly Father would do all things well, and that in his own good time and way, he would come to her deliverance. Never before had she felt such perfect resignation to his will, never such per-fect confidence in his power and mercy.

The meeting closed and the ladies repaired to the audience room, which was already well filled. Seats had been reserved for them in the body of of the church in front of the speaker's platform. So soon as they were seated the president called the meeting to order and introduced the lecturer of the evening. As he came forward a feeling of disappointment was evidently apparent throughout the audience. He was an entire stranger, never having been seen in Cedarville before. His appearance was unprepossessing. His head was large and covered with a thick growth of sandy hair, just beginning to turn gray. His age appeared to be about fifty. His dress was plain in the extreme. After for a moment, surveying the audience, he began his address. His voice was low and solemn, scarce-ly being heard at the farther end of room, but instantly every voice was hushed, and in trem-ulous tones he proceeded.

*"My friends, did you ever see a beautiful

*For much that is contained in this address, the author is indebted to a little volume, read when he was a boy, entitled: "Why am I a Temperance Man."

ship leaving her port for some foreign shore, with every stitch of canvas set, her flag waving at the mast-head, her beautiful streamers floating out on the breeze? Sailing away with the bright sunbeams playing around her, amid the waiving of handkershiefs and the joyous good-byes of those who remain on the shore? Sailing away upon the ocean freighted with the hopes and joys of years to come? Even so, years long gone, was my barque launched upon the sea of life, and with high hopes and bright prospects I commenced that voyage which all must take, and which none may take but once. Have you seen that same proud ship come back, scarcely entering the harbor, her banners gone, her streamers carried away, with torn sails and dismantled rigging, almost a wreck, yet saved at last? Even so you see before you, one who has passed through the storms, and though at last has found a refuge of safety, will carry with him to the tomb the sad evidence of the conflict with the storm."

He paused, and there was the silence of death. In those few words he had won every heart. Again he spoke, and his voice fell in soft cadence on every ear of the vast audience.

"I have come to-night to tell you something of my past experience, in the hope that it may either warn some of my fellow voyagers of the rocks on which I so nearly stranded, or encourage others in the hour of their danger, to

turn their eye to the star of Bethlehem, whose
light at last guided me to the port of peace."

Then for more than an hour he held his audience spell-bound, often moving them to tears,
as he told of his early hopes, his bright prospects
for usefulness, of his marriage and happy joyous home, of his fall through the influence of
drink, his degredation, and how, at last, when
all hope seemed gone, when all had forsaken
him but his faithful, devoted wife, her faithful-
ness was rewarded and her prayers answered.
"If," he continued, "there is one blessing for
for which, more than another, I feel thankful,
it is that I am saved from the power of rum.
Next to this is the blessing that my deliverance
was effected before the dear, devoted wife was
called to cross the river of death. She lived to
see me reclaimed. She heard my voice lifted in
warning accents to those who were yet battling
with the storm. When death came and laid on
her his cold hand, with a sweet smile of resignation, she laid her head upon my heart and
winding her cold arm around my neck said:
'Now let death come, I am ready.' The one purpose for which, for years, she had lived, was
accomplished. We laid her away in the blessed
sleep of the righteous, and over her new made
grave I planted the flowers and renewed my vows
of consecration to my life work, saving my fellow
men. Wherever I go I seem to feel around me
the gentle, holy influence of her presence. And

oh! if to-night her spirit is permitted to look down from her bright and beautiful home on high, among all the scenes of earth on which her eye can rest, there is none that makes her Heaven so joyful as that of her husband seeking to save those who, like himself, has fallen beneath the power of the tempter. And why may we not believe it is so?' Is there not 'joy among the angels of God over one sinner that repenteth?'

"Let me appeal especially to those who fear they have passed beyond the power of redemption. There are none here to-night, there can possibly be none, who have fallen lower than I had, or whose condition appears more hopeless. The same Divine hand that reached down to my wretchedness and lifted me up, is to-night outstretched to you. Do not depend on your own strength for your deliverance, but on that of Him who came to seek and to save the lost. Do not, however, let me undervalue the greatness of your own strength. There is a mighty power even in a determined human effort; but a determined human effort made in the strength of God, becomes invincible. There is a mighty power in a solemn pledge. Here, perhaps, is where some of you have made a mistake. It is one of the rocks on which I so nearly stranded. I fancied I could as well keep from drinking without signing a pledge as with it. How sadly I was mistaken, my long years of shame and sorrow sadly testify. So long as I refused to sign a pledge and connect myself with a temperance society, so long I was the victim of every one who choose to tempt me. But when I signed and was solemnly pledged to total abstinence, then no honorable man would ask me to break my pledge. This, my friends, .was the first step in my reformation. But it was not until I cast my poor, helpless broken spirit on God, that I felt I was saved. I am here to-night, saved from the sad fate of a drunkard, because I signed a pledge never to taste another drop of liquor, and because I am constantly depending in humble reliance on. Divine power for strength to keep that pledge. If there be here to-night, a poor inebriate who would fain break the tempter's chain, to you I extend my hand and say, 'come thou and do likewise.'"

He closed his address and the pledge was produced. One after another came forward and wrote their names, until about thirty had affixed their signatures. Presently a murmur ran through the audience. It grew louder, as a manly form was seen to pass up the aisle and take his place by the table. Sherwood saw him, and with and audible "Thank God," bowed his head in silent prayer. Mrs. Wardsworth was sitting with her head resting on the back of the seat, with throbbing heart pleading with God. Mrs. Thornton, who was sitting by

her side, called her attention, and quickly
drying her eyes she looked up. Her husband
was standing at the table. Taking up the pen,
he slowly and deliberately dipped it in the ink,
and in a clear, bold hand traced the name of
"Harry Wardsworth." The audience was
hushed to silence. A solemn awe pervaded the
entire assembly. The pastor of the church
was the first to recover himself, and rising, he
said, "Let us pray," and with a voice which
betrayed the deep emotion of his soul, he
prayed that God would impart strength to
carry out every resolution and to keep sacred
every vow. A few more came forward and
affixed their signatures to the pledge, the
audience joined in singing "Praise God from
whom all blessings flow," the benediction was
pronounced and the audience dispersed. Several came forward and warmly grasping
Wardsworth's hand, wished him God speed,
but for himself, his emotions were too deep for
utterance. To his wife, the whole scene
appeared like a pleasant dream. She could
hardly believe the evidence of her own senses. So
seldom is it that we are prepared to receive the
blessing when it comes, or to recognize the
answer to our prayers.

But few words were spoken during the walk
home. It was not until the wife had gained the
privacy of her own room that she felt free to
let the deep fountains of her gratitude overflow

and offer the burden of her thanks. There she knelt, and in that moment of communion, all the past, with its hours, its weeks, nay, its years of darkness and sorrow was forgotten. The burden that for years had been crushing her to the earth, rolled off and fell into that sepulchre where was already buried the grief of the past. The long dark night with its darkness and its gloom was ended. The morning of hope and joy had at last dawned. Slowly all this great truth came to her. Out of the dead past she stepped into the living present! The shadows were departing. Afar off she could trace them, but swifter and swifter were they receding before the advancing morning All the pain of the past was forgotten in the bliss of the present. Oh! the joy of that moment. There was but one thought and that filled all her soul. Her prayers were answered and her husband was reclaimed.

Not for one moment did she doubt either his determination or strength to keep inviolate his pledge. He had at last reached the high ground to which she had so long turned her tearful eyes. God had heard her prayer, and granted her that much, and she received it as but the assurance that the same Divine power would aid in accomplishing the rest.

Great, however, as was her surprise and joy, a still greater awaited. her. She returned to the sitting room to meet her husband, but he was not there. She repaired to the chamber, and there, in the room, lightened only by the beams of the bright, full moon, as it shone through the window, she found him. In low, tremulous tones, he was pleading for Divine help to keep inviolate the pledge he had taken. But what pen shall describe that struggle? It was the turning point in Harry Wardsworth's life, and he well knew it. He must conquer now or go down into the deep, dark current, whose dismal waters are ever dashing upon the shore where there is no hope. It was the last desperate struggle of the strong man for his life, the last desperate struggle of the monster for his victim. It was a moment of awful sublimity. As his wife, with streaming eyes and throbbing heart, watched the struggle, she could only cry from the depths of her spirit. "Lord hear and save." Kneeling by his side she united her prayers with his, and together their petitions ascended to the throne of the Eternal.

Presently his voice grew strangely calm. A hand Divine was outstretched, and by faith he grasped it. His prayer had been heard, and the voice that re-echoed over the stormy waves of Geneseret's lake had whispered to the raging tempest of his soul, "Peace! be still." The Divine spirit came down and sealed the forgiveness upon his heart, and a Father's loving arms enfolded the returning prodigal.

When he arose and came forth from that chamber, his face wore a look that never rested there before. It was a look of calm, holy peace and trust. It spoke, as plainly as words could utter it, "He has found the refuge, henceforth he is safe." He went into the chamber an earnest, supplicating penitent; he came out a forgiven child, a saved man.

Together they repaired to the sitting room, and there we will leave them. That hour of sacred, holy communion with themselves and God is too sacred for curious eyes to look upon. Enough to say, the Comforter was there, and the angel of peace spread his pinons over and around them, and "There was joy in the presence of the angels over another sinner who had repented."

CHAPTER XII.

Many, indeed, were the opinons expressed in regard to Harry Wardsworth signing the pledge, and the prospect of his complete recovery from the vice of drunkenness. As usual, those opinions were as varied as were the numbers that held them, and their expression served to illustrate their good or ill will toward Wardsworth him self.

Some, but unfortunately they were in the minority, saw in the act the assurance of hope, and resolved to aid to the extent of their ability. Others hoped the reformation might be permanent, but greatly feared the result, knowing well the fearful hold which the destroyer had taken of his victim. Others still, not only refused to believe in the genuineness of his reformation, but showed too plainly, that in their case, the wish was father to the thought. Among the latter were Simkins and Slocum. The former of those gentlemen remembered but too vividly for his own pleasure, the influence which Wardsworth had possessed in the days of his strength, and the part he (Simkins) had taken in his ruin, and very much feared that possibly retribution might at some time be visited upon his own head.

"The trouble with that class of men," said the Hon (?) gentleman, "is, their honor is gone. They have no principle of honor. There is nothing to build on. I have no doubt but Wardsworth means well, and at times would like to become a sober man; but the trouble is, he has given up his manhood, thrown away his honor, and what are you going to do in such a case?" Another illustration of "Satin rebuking sin."

Walter Pitman, the very respectable saloonkeeper, to whom the reader has already been introduced, gave his opinion without any hesitation, and openly boasted of his determination to entrap Wardsworth and induce him to violate his pledge.

"I tell you what it is, gentleman," he remarked to a number of his customers, "I have seen just such things before. Hank Wardsworth won't keep his pledge three months, or my name ain't Walt Pitman."

"What makes you think that?" asked one of his listeners.

"O, let Walt alone for that," was the answer, as he gave a knowing wink. "Wait till I get hold of him. If I don't get him to drink the first time I get a chance, then I'll treat all hands I have seen lots of such cases, and I never failed yet in getting them to drink when I once went about it."

In this case, however, the crafty saloon keeper did more than he intended. Among the listeners present was Joe Bliss, a man who had once been comparatively wealthy and respected, but who had reached almost the lowest level of drunkenness.

The cool, deliberate manner in which Pitman boasted of his plans for Wardsworth's more complete ruin, affected him strangely. Springing from his seat, he walked up to the bar, behind which Pitman was standing, and looking the saloon keeper in the face, asked:

"Do you mean to say, Pitman, that if you could, you would get Wardsworth to break his pledge?"

"Certainly, I mean to say so. It is my business to sell liquor; that is what I pay the license for. Don't I pay the government a good big price for the privilege of selling liquor, and do you think I am such a fool as to let everybody sign the pledge and become sober, and thus break up my own business, if I can help it? What do you say to that, old man?"

"I say it is the most infernal business ever a man engaged in; and anybody who will try to get Harry Wardsworth to violate a solemn pledge, and lead him again to drunkenness, is worse than a thief, I do not care how great a claim he lays to respectability. That's my opinion, Walter Pitman."

The wiley saloonist saw his mistake and at once tried to correct it. Looking at Bliss with one of his most winning smiles, he answered :

"I know what is wrong with you, Joe ; you have not had your bitters this morning!" and turning to where the liquors were kept, he added —"come, what'll you take?"

"*Nothing!*" thundered Joe.

"What ! nothing?"

"No ; nothing from you," and looking steadly into the face of the saloon keeper, he continued :

"Say, Pitman, did you ever know Joe Bliss to do a mean thing?"

"No, Joe," was the reply, "I never knew you to do a mean thing in your life."

"No ; I thought not; and you might have added, that you never knew me to do a good one. But now I am going to do one, yes, two· good acts. First, I am going directly to Harry Wardsworth and warn him that you have deliberately planned to induce him to break his pledge; and second, I am going to sign the same pledge that Wardsworth has, and if there is any honor left in Joe Bliss, I am going to keep it ;" and he walked out leaving the saloon keeper the most disconcerted man in Cedarville. For once the Devil had reckoned without his host, as that was the last time ever Joe Bliss visited a whisky saloon.

As for Solomon Slocum, Esquire, there was but one thing that troubled him. That was not his conscience, for he had got a long way beyond any trouble from that direction.

As we have seen, Mrs. Wardsworth had never signed the deed he had so fraudulently obtained from her husband; and in the absence of her signature, a cloud rested on his title to the property. He had fully believed that Wardsworth would be either hung or imprisoned, in which case he hoped to take advantage of her circumstances and induce her for a few dollars, to sign the deed. But the acquittal of her husband, and especially his reformation had sadly interfered with his plans, and he began to fear, not only that he would fail to perfect his title, but that he might be made to suffer the penalty of his crimes.

It is not then surprising that his first act on hearing that Wardsworth had signed the pledge, was to call on his bosom friend and counsellor, Hon. Hezekiah Simkins.

"I say, Simkins," he remarked, "what is to be done about my title to that property I got of Wardsworth?"

"What do you mean, Slocum?" answered the lawyer; "have you not got your deed, regularly executed by Wardsworth? Has he not given you possession, and you are now living in the house? What more do you want?"

"True, but you are aware that his wife never.

signed the deed. That is what troubles me now."

"Very true; I thought you were foolish in not making an effort to secure her signature while her husband was in prison."

"I see it now, and only wish I had taken your advice; but I was sure Wardsworth would either be hung or sent to prison, in which case poverty would have come to my aid. There is nothing like starvation, you know, to bring proud people to terms."

"But you see he was neither hung nor sent to prison, and from present appearances, I do not see much prospect of either one happening. However, I do not believe there is any danger of Wardsworth giving you any trouble. If he does, I have helped you out of some very tough scrapes, as you know, and I guess I can see you through this."

"Oh, I don't fear on his account. Old Slocum was too cunning to set a trap for himself; besides, he wont care to go back and dig up his own degradation, and he knows that the transaction was legal, if it was not just as one would wish to be done by; but what I now want is to work some way to secure her signature to the deed."

"Well, Slocum, there is but one course open to you, so far as I can see, and that is to come down handsomely and make an offer that will be worth her while to accept."

The result of the above conversation was,

that a few days after, Wardsworth received from Simkins the following note:

CEDARVILLE, ——, 18—.

HARRY WARDSWORTH, Esq.:

Dear Sir:—You are no doubt aware that the signature of Mrs. Wardsworth has never yet been obtained to the deed you gave to Solomon Slocum, of the property on Maple avenue. I am instructed by Mr. S. to say he would like her signature to complete his title, and, if she insists on it, is willing to pay any reasonable amount for the trouble it may cause her.

Truly yours,

H. SIMKINS.

To this note, the lawyer received the following reply:

CEDARVILLE, ——, 18—.

H. SIMKINS, Esq.:

Dear Sir:—My wife instructs me to say to you that she declines to become a party to the deed referred to, preferring not to be associated in any way with the transaction.

I add for myself, you may assure your client, that personally, I shall give him no trouble, preferring to let that matter sleep, with other similar transactions, in the grave of the buried past. Truly yours,

H. WARDSWORTH.

And thus the matter of the home was settled

and Slocum's avarice in a measure was satisfied.

Three months went by, during which Wards-worth faithfully kept his pledge, and constantly implored Divine aid in carrying out his resolutions. And when, at the end of that time, he knelt at the altar and received from the minister of Christ, the sacred emblems of a Savior's death, and was publicly admitted to the fellowship and communion of Christ's church, it was generally admitted that he had indeed entered on a higher plane of life, and that his reformation was complete.

To himself that day was destined to be one of the most eventful in his life. In company with his wife, he had twice attended church, and at the close of the evening service had walked with his friend Thornton to the residence of that gentleman, where were spent a couple of hours in earnest conversation. The past was calmly reviewed, and the future looked to with hope. Suddenly, as they conversed, the room grew lighter. A moment more and there was heard the cry of fire, and, at the same instant, there rang out the clear, warning notes of the fire bell, calling the brave firemen to their terrible conflict with the angry element.

"Where is the fire?" asked Thornton, as in company with Wardsworth he gained the street.

"Slocum's distillery," was the answer, and a hundred voices seemed to take up the answer and echo it—"Slocum's distillery." Then there was a hurrying of feet in wild confusion, and soon a hundred willing men, foremost among whom was the man Slocum had so deeply wronged, were ready to battle with the devouring foe.

The building, which was wholly of wood, was soon enveloped in flames, and before the fire engines arrived all hope of saving it was gone. Still fiercer raged the fire—the flames sending forth their long, forked tongues, hissing and roaring as though a thousand angry demons were holding high carnival. They burst from the windows, they wrapped themselves around the external walls, they darted high up into the midnight darkness, they reached far out like the arm of some avenging foe, outstretched to grasp his victim.

Nobly indeed did both firemen and citizens do their duty. The most gigantic efforts were put forth, but all to no purpose; the building and its contents were all alike doomed, and the hour of its destruction had come.

Presently a confused murmur, at first vague and undefined, ran through the crowd. Soon it took form and was passed from one to another, every countenance turning pale as the words fell on the ear—"Slocum's two sons are in the building." On inquiry, it was learned that in company with one or two others, they had spent the evening in the office playing cards. The office was in the second story, near where the fire had first been discovered. They were intoxicated and refused to go home, saying they would sleep in the office. This was all that could be learned.

At that moment, in another part of the building, a window was suddenly broken from the inside, and the ghastly face of one was seen in the very midst of the flames preparing to jump to the ground. But before he could accomplish his purpose a sheet of flame came down with a whirl and a roar, and striking him full in the face, literally hurled him back into the burning building. The next moment the roof fell with a terrible crash, and the sons were engulfed in the sea of fire, while higher and fiercer mounted the flames, as if in mad revelry over the fearful triumph they had achieved.

Suddenly, in the midst of the commotion, the form of Slocum was seen approaching with all the speed he could command, his countenance distorted with rage and excitement, and giving vent to the most blasphemous curses. His eyes possessed that peculiarly wild look sometimes seen in sudden and violent insanity. The foam lay out on the corners of his mouth, and his full face seemed fuller and had assumed the color of dark purple. By the time he had reached the scene of destruction he was overcome, and with one terrible curse he fell to the ground in a state of entire insensibility. They

ran and raised him up, while two or three
physicians who were present went to his aid;
but a speedy examination revealed the hopelessness of the case, and instructions were
immediately given for his removal to his home.
They conveyed him back to his house and did
all that science and skill could accomplish to
avert the impending fate; but it was evident to
all that the day of his retribution had come, and
as the flickering flames died out from the ruins
of the doomed manufactory of death, the spirit
of its owner went up to its account before the
God against whom he had so long and so griev-
ously sinned.

When the ruins had sufficiently cooled to
permit it, they gathered all that was left of the
bones of the dead sons, and, with the form of
the dead father, they were laid in one grave in
Rosebloom cemetery. The career of Solomon
Slocum had closed in the darkness of death, and
few indeed were the mourners who wept.

But alas for the wife and mother, who had
always possessed a refined and sensitive nature,
all too much so for her own happiness, as the
wife of such a man as Slocum. On her the
calamity of his death and that of the sons, fell
with crushing force, from the effect of which
she never rallied. As some sensitive flower,
touched by the sudden and early frost perishes,
so she drooped, and at the end of two months
the messenger came and folded her to rest.

Another procession was formed, another grave was opened, and Rosebloom cemetery received yet another victim of the rum traffic. Again had the innocent been made to suffer for the sins of the guilty, but over against the whole was written, "The judgments of the Lord are true and righteous altogether."

CHAPTER . XIII.

SUNSHINE.

Time in its ever restless march has swiftly passed, heedless alike of the joys and sorrows, the happy spirits and broken hearts which it has passed in its swift course. Three years more have elapsed, and once more, and for the last time, we visit the beautiful city of Cedarville.

To the city, as well as to many of its inhabitants, those three years have brought many changes. Old familiar forms have vanished, and in their stead appear new faces. There is the same restless activity that characterizes all our growing western cities, but Cedarville appears different from what it did when we last visited it. Then it wore an appearance of neglect. Its streets were uncared for and many of its buildings were more or less dilapidated. Now everything seemed changed for the better. The streets are neatly cleaned, many of the old buildings replaced with new and more imposing structures, and the whole city shows evidence of being on the high road to prosperity.

One class of buildings we miss, and at once our interest is aroused. *The corner saloon is gone.* The low, dirty looking buildings, with red curtains at the windows and green painted screens just within the door, are conspicuous by their absence. At once we define the cause of the change, and as we think of those whom we knew so well, and remember their bitter struggles or their terrible retribution, we pause, overcome by a flood of painful emotion.

Instinctively we turn toward the place where once stood Slocum's distillery, and where we last saw the lurid flames enwrap the doomed building. Approaching the spot we see a large and costly brick stucture. From its tall chimney the black smoke is issuing, while from two or three exhaust pipes the white steam belches forth as if conscious of its power and usefulness. On a large, wide sign board, running the whole length of the roof, we read, "CEDARVILLE AGRICULTURAL WORKS." It is the hour of noon. The whistle sounds, and forthwith there comes from within its walls a hundred sturdy men, their strong, sinewy arms bare to the elbows, their faces covered with the dust of honest toil, and, with quick, firm step each one goes his way to the home where cheerful faces wait to greet him.

There is no longer any doubt as to the cause of the changed appearance of the city. The absence of the distillery and saloon, the presence of so large a factory where honest toil can pursue its course unhindered by the debasing and destroying influence of rum, is sufficient explanation for all the changes so noticeable in Cedarville.

One building especially attracts our attention. It is a handsome and imposing structure standing directly on the corner, where, three years ago stood Sweney's saloon.

It is a large, new wholesale store, built a year ago by Mr. Sherwood; and from one of the windows of the second story there hangs out a beautiful and attractive sign bearing the names of "Ferguson & Wardsworth, attorneys at law."

Two years previously the lovers of law and order had made another vigorous effort to secure the passage of a prohibitory liquor law for the city, and had succeeded even beyond their own expectations. The no license ticket had been carried in Cedarville by such an overwhelming majority that the saloon keepers and their friends saw how hopeless it would be longer to continue the fight, most of them either gave up the business or removed to other and more congenial communities. Some few remained, resolved to defy the law, but the sentiment of the people was against them, and after one or two fines and imprisonments, they too gave up the unequal strife and departed for a different moral atmosphere.

At the request of Wardsworth and others, Ferguson had visited the city and spent a week in aiding the temperance party in their agitation; and when the battle was ended and the victory won, he was induced to join Wardsworth, who had already regained the greater part of his popularity and practice, in prosecuting a more extensive business.

The names of Ferguson & Wardsworth had already become a tower of strength. The suffering and oppressed ever found in them safe counsellors and friends. A year had not passed since their union in business till they become the acknowledged leaders at the bar of the State. Remembering all the past, they lived and labored together, not merely for what money they could make, but for the good they were enabled to do.

To Wardsworth and his home those years have brought sunshine in more ways than one. After the death of Slocum, his property passed into the hands of his creditors, and in due course was offered for sale. On investigation it was found that the assets were more than sufficient to pay all the claims against the estate, with the cost of administration, without the necessity of the creditors bidding in any of the property. And so it happened when the resi-

dence on Maple avenue was offered, the public
remembering pretty well how Slocum became
possessed of it, and knowing that a cloud still
rested on the title, were either too generous to
take it from the rightful owner, or too timid to
risk their money on uncertainty; and when it
was "knocked down," for three thousand dollars,
it was found that Thos. Sherwood, acting on
behalf of Harry Wardsworth, had become the
purchaser.

To have the deed made in Wardsworth's
name, and to put him in possession, was but the
work of a few days, and so to the devoted wife
the sunshine grew brighter and brighter, and
once more her cheerful songs awoke the echoes
within the walls of the home that had been
alike the witness of her greatest joy and
deepest sorrow.

The sun still lingers in the west, as if loth to
leave a scene of such hallowed peace and beauty,
as we stroll along Maple avenue to take one
lingering look at the home of the Wardsworths.
The home and grounds are but little changed,
but what change there is, is for the better. All
the wood work has been newly painted and
grounds nicely laid off, while the fragrance of
early blooming flowers greet us as we approach,
and seemingly invite us to enter.

Seated on the veranda is a man of apparently
middle age, who, though changed since last we
met him, we recognize as Harry Wardsworth.

His countenance wears a look of thoughtful cheerfulness, and ever and anon lights up with a smile at some pleasant remark from his wife, who sits just within the opened window, where she can carry on the conversation with her husband, and at the same time, keep her eye on a second "Little Harry," who has come to add his quota of blessing to the already happy parents. From the husband's brow the dark locks are thrown back, revealing here and there a few threads of silver, which speak more of life struggles than of age.

. The reader need not be told that Wardsworth has faithfully kept his pledge. With his feet planted upon the rock of Eternal strength, he has been enabled to hurl defiance at his foe, and has come off conqueror.

With his wife the change is more marked than with himself. We can hardly believe her to be the same pale, care-worn woman of three years ago. The old smile has returned, and though the traces of the fires through which she has passed yet remain, it is evident they have but consumed the dross, while the pure gold has come forth from the furnace refined and purified.

In her hand she holds a letter which she has been reading to her husband. Using an author's pivilege, we glance at the neatly traced page, and read as follows:

CEDARVILLE,———,18—.

Dear Sister Kate,—Although it is not long since I wrote you, I am impelled by the fullness of my heart to address you once again. I write not only for my own sake, but on Harry's behalf as well.

I am forcibly reminded of that sad letter I penned to you, now nearly four years ago, and as I remember the past and realize the present, it all seems like some dream, and I can hardly believe I have passed through sorrow's dark night, so bright and beautiful appears the morning.

I have told you, in a former letter, how we became re-possessed of our beautiful home. I must tell you now that Harry has paid the last dollar of claim, and this dear home is ours once more. Harry has explained all about that hundred and fifty dollars, and I know whence it came, and while my heart goes out in loving gratitude to you, my dear sister, both for my sake and husband's please accept the inclosed draft in payment of principal and interest.

Now, dear sister, pemit me to ask once more, can you not come and visit me. Harry says if you will, I may go back home with you, and I will. I long to see you all, but first I want you to come and share my joy.

As I think of all the way "a Father's hand has led me," I am ready to exclaim with Israel's psalmist of old, "Thou annointst my head with oil, my cup runneth over." I am convinced that one reason why so many wives fail in their efforts to reclaim their husbands, is because, either they do not let their prayers and efforts go hand in hand, or else their faith fails them and they too quickly yield in the struggle. Be this as it may; for me, I will ever render the tribute of my gratitude, that though we have passed through the shadows, we have reached the sunshine at last.   SISTER BELLE.

CHAPTER XIV.

CONCLUSION.

Thus ends our simple story. We trust that our readers have not only been interested, but that they have been instructed and benefiitted as well, by thus getting a clearer insight into the workings of the liquor traffic—this most deadly foe to all that is good and pure in the home circle. Would, dear reader, that this were merely a story of fiction—that the scenes here pictured, existed only in our imagination. But, unfortunately, this is not so. In many of those scenes the author has, either as a physician or a minister, been called to bear a painful part. He can bear testimony, not only that they are true, but that one-half the sad truth has not been written. It is a story of temptation and trial—of sinning and suffering—of disappointment and despair—of ruin and remorse—such as finds its counterpart in thousands of American homes at the present day. No pen of fiction can write the lines, no pencil of artist can drape the scenes, in a manner to do the subject justice.

Doubtless many, whose eyes may trace these pages, will, themselves—perhaps all too sadly —recognize the pictures we have drawn, the histories we have written. We ask, are they not, alas! too true to life? Is not the whole history of the liquor traffic a history of broken hearts, of blasted hopes, of blighted prospects, of physical and mental wrecks? Is not its record a record of crimes committed, of fortunes wasted, of health and happiness destroyed, and paupers and criminals multiplied? Has it not written its history with the blood of the millions it has slain, and paved its pathway with the dead bodies of its murdered victims?

Sanctioned and protected by legal enactments, with whom it has joined hands in its cruel warfare against the weak and defenseless, and courted by political parties for its power in elections, has it not gone on, filling our poor houses with its paupers, our asylums with its lunatics, our prisons with its criminals, our cemeteries with its dead, and the whole land with bitter lamentation and woe?

Alas! that in our otherwise free and enlight-

ened America such things should be! That in
ten thousand cities, towns and villages, throughout this country, claiming to be a christian
land, there are written daily, just such sad life
histories, as the result of the legalized liquor
traffic. That in this christian land, from seventy to a hundred thousand citizens are slain
every year, and this wholesale destruction of
human life, is sanctioned by the people for a
money consideration.

Disguise the truth as we may, or seek to evade
its force, the awful fact stares us in the face,
that, besides the untold misery and anguish it
produces, the paupers, idiots, lunatics and criminals it sends forth, the American people are,
through this traffic, sanctioning the annual
murder of from seventy to a hundred thousand
of our citizens evey year for a money consideration.

Does the reader reply, "This is a strong
statement?" We admit it, and sorrow because,
that strong as it is, it is more than justified by
the facts. Does not the saloon-keeper engage
in this unrighteous business, well knowing its
death-dealing influences, because of the large
profits derived from his sales? A profit said to
exceed eighty per cent. Do not the city
councils license the saloon-keeper, because of
the money it puts into the treasury? Do not
the people sanction the granting of those
licenses, because the fund thus raised, lightens

their financial burdens and lessens the amount of their taxes? Does not the general government permit the manufacture of the liquor because of the revenue derived therefrom? Do not the people support the government in thus permitting its manufacture, for a money consideration, because the revenue thus derived lessens direct taxation? Is not every argument against the manufacture and sale of this destructive agency, met with the counter argument, that the country needs and must have this revenue? Is it claimed that the American people delight in this human misery and suffering, and continue that which produces them, simply for the pleasure which the suffering affords them? In short, would all this wholesale destruction of fortune and reason and happiness and human life, be continued for a single day, were it not for the financial benefit, it is claimed the country derives from the manufacture and sale of that which destroys? We submit that the most charitable view which we can reasonably take of this subject, is the view we have here taken; and that no statement or fact can be more clearly proven, than that the American people are sanctioning this wholesale destruction of human life, for a money consideration.*

*In this statement the author would censure himself equally with others. So strong have been his party affiliations, that it has taken him a lifetime to learn the lesson of duty.

And what of its future? This is the one great question of the day; before which all other questions of state policy sink into insignificance. A question that will be neither thrust aside, nor satisfied with an evasive answer. A question that it is neither wise, nor just now humane, for any party or state longer to evade. A question that must be settled, and that can only be permanently settled in one way—and this in a way to meet the approval of an enlightened human conscience, and the dictates of justice and humanity.

It remains for the American people to say— because *the will of the people is law*—whether this mighty torrent of human degradation and death shall be permitted to flow on, or whether they will arise in the strength of their might and arrest it. If it continues in the future, as in the past, annually to bear this great army of ruined, murdered victims, on its dark and dismal current, out to a darker and more dismal eternity beyond, it will be because either the people so decree it, or remain indifferent spectators of the scene, while the work of destruction goes on.

Let one fact be remembered, and act as a stimulant in this great conflict. Not a single home is safe. Not a single family can claim positive exemption. Your own dear boy, the pride of your life, may yet be overtaken by the destroyer and slain, or your own dear girl, the

idol of your heart, and the sunlight of your
home, may yet sit with weeping eyes and breaking heart, amid the desolations, caused by the
traffic which your influence has sustained.
Amid such a sorrow, of what significance will
be the question of the tariff, or any other of the
hundred questions, designing politicians would
lead us to believe must be settled, before we can
stop to save the husbands, brothers, sons and
neighbors of our land from the terrible destruction everywhere overtaking them?

What say you, reader, holding in your hand
that mightiest of all civil forces, the ballot of
an American voter?   What say you, desolate
father, standing over the grave of your first born,
ruined and murdered by rum, that your neighbor might save a few dollars in his school taxes?
What say you, heart-broken mother, looking out
into the midnight darkness, for the coming of
your boy, whose feet have already been "*lured
by the law*" into the way of death?   What say
you, stricken wife, as you turn from the grave of
the father of your children, slain by the legalized liquor traffic, and the price of whose blood
has been paid into the treasury?   What say
you, oh christian, who, for a few paltry pence,
saved in your school taxes, would thus put destruction in your brother's path?   What say
you, one and all?   Shall we who boast of being
a free people, remain longer in bondage to such
a tyrant?   Or shall we rise, and, in the name

of God and humanity, hurl the monster from
our shores, and resolve to protect our country
and our homes?

Hark!! The answer comes back to us. It is
heard in that wail of anguish that comes
from those seventy thousand desolate homes.
It comes borne upon the breeze as it sighs a low
sad requiem over those seventy thousand dishonored graves. It is heard in that unmistak-
able murmur of indignation and resolve that is
heard from the Atlantic to the Pacific, from
Minnesota to the Gulf of Mexico. We read the
answer in the marshaling of the mighty host,
clad in the panoply of truth, and resolved in
God's name to conquer. They have heard the
clarion note, calling them to battle, and, gird-
ing on their armor, are rallying to the watch-
word PROHIBITION. From Northern vales and
Southern glades; from Eastern hills and
Western plains they come. Led on by a thousand societies, who for years have laid broad and
deep the foundation of those principles, for the
establishment of which the battle rages. In the
front ranks, behold a great array of noble women,
who have gathered for the conflict, and on whose
banners is inscribed in letters of living light,
"For God and Home and Native Land." From
a hundred thousand homes, in which hope
again succeeds to blank espai , is heard the
pleading prayer, "God bless and speed them on
their mission." State after state has already

caught the inspiration of a great principle, and their camp fires are brightly burning to cheer their comrades, as they rally for the coming conflict.

And what shall be the answer of our state? —of all the states? What shall be the answer of our country—of my country? The country of my adoption, the country of my home. To me fairer than my own native land—than any other land under the sun. With a history more precious, and a future more promising than any other nation on the globe. Would to God, that America might lead the van in this grand forward movement, and set an example for the rest of the nations to follow.

Let every christian but act, in this matter, from the standpoint of true religion. Let every citizen be governed by the truest principles of patriotism. Let all the people unite to carry out the noblest principles of political economy. Let this be done, and half a decade will not pass, till our country shall come up, out of the deep dark shadows, that have so long enshrouded her, into the bright and beautiful sunshine of that day, foretold by the prophetic bard, ages ago, when "The voice of weeping shall be no more heard in the land, nor the voice of cursing. There shall no more be thence an infant of days, nor an old man who has not filled his days, for the child shall die an hundred years old. They shall build houses and inhabit them. They shall plant vineyards and eat the fruit of them. They shall not build, and another inhabit; they shall not plant and another eat the fruit thereof, for as the days of a tree shall be the days of my people."

THE END.